Out
in Left
Field

Out in Left Field

by DON LEMNA

illustrated by MATT COLLINS

Holiday House / New York

For Pat, my brother

Text copyright © 2012 by Don Lemna
Illustrations copyright © 2012 by Matt Collins
All Rights Reserved
HOLIDAY HOUSE is registered in the U.S. Patent and Trademark Office.
Printed and Bound in November 2012 at Maple Vail, York, PA, USA.
www.holidayhouse.com

3   5   7   9   10   8   6   4   2

Library of Congress Cataloging-in-Publication Data
Lemna, Don, 1936–
Out in left field / Don Lemna ; [illustrations by Matt Collins].
p. cm.
Sequel to: When the sergeant came marching home.
Summary: Eleven-year-old Donald thinks nothing could be worse than missing a pop fly in
a baseball game that most of his Montana town was watching, but through the end of 1947
and beginning of 1948, he suffers one humiliation after another.
ISBN 978-0-8234-2313-2 (hardcover)
[1. Farm life—Montana—Fiction.   2. Family life—Montana—Fiction.   3. Montana—
History—20th century—Fiction.]   I. Collins, Matt, ill.   II. Title.
PZ7.L53766Out 2012
[Fic]—dc23
2011040625
ISBN 978-0-8234-2766-6 (paperback)

Contents

CHAPTER ONE
The Big Game

It was August 1947, the beginning of our second year on the farm, with long summer days and our fields of wheat ripening in the hot Montana sun. And there I was, eleven years old and for once I didn't have a care in the world. Then Rachel came along with a note in her hand—a summons to doom and destruction that was to ruin my life forever.

Rachel lived in the white farmhouse down the road from us—along with her parents, Mr. and Mrs. Schneider, and her various sisters, of whom there were four at last count.

"It's from Miss Scott," she said. Miss Scott was our teacher.

I opened the note and read:

The Summer Get-Together with Melody School will be held on Saturday, August 14, at the Station Hill School. Bring a picnic lunch. The volleyball and baseball games will begin at 2 pm, after lunch. There will be a practice for our teams in Station Hill on Thursday at 1 pm.

Miss Scott

Just before school ended, Miss Scott told us that she'd made the arrangements for the Get-Together with Mrs. Lemelin, who taught in a one-room, eight-grade school like ours in the nearby town of Melody.

After her announcement there was a lot of bragging from the boys about how we would soon teach the Melodies how to play baseball.

"It doesn't matter who wins the games," Miss Scott solemnly warned us. "The objective is to have fun and get to know our neighbors."

"I already know them," Billy Shapiro declared. "And they stink at baseball!"

Henry Adamson, a formidable grade-seven kid, ran the show as far as our baseball was concerned. He had organized the boys who played—which was nearly everyone from grade three up—into two well-balanced teams. Henry was the biggest kid in the school. There are good big kids and bad big kids, and Henry was one of the good ones. He was fair-minded, and he was a born leader. We all looked up to him.

Henry loved baseball, and he took our little noon-hour scrub games very seriously. From his catcher's position on the Blue team, he controlled the play and kept us all on the straight and narrow. He also looked after the equipment, which consisted of a few bats and balls, a catcher's mitt, and a collection of baseball gloves that looked like they'd been through the War of 1812.

Henry had selected the team to represent us against Melody, and much to my surprise, I was on it.

"I'm on the volleyball team," Rachel proudly reminded me when I'd finished reading the note. She jumped in the air as though she were spiking a ball. "Daddy's taking everyone in on the bus," she said as she left for home.

I was looking forward to the game against Melody. Even though I'd only started playing baseball last year when we moved to the Station Hill area, I already loved the game. A lot was expected of me too, because everyone at school knew that my uncle Danny had been a semiprofessional baseball player and that he would have made it into the big leagues if the Second World War hadn't come along.

They knew about my uncle Danny because I'd told them. This was a big mistake. Ever since I'd mentioned it, I'd been mocked and teased about it by Axel Smart.

Axel was in my grade. He played center field on the Blue team, right next to me, and he never missed an opportunity to use my stupid boast about my uncle to belittle me.

If I missed a catch, Axel would wave his finger at me and shout, "Hey, Donald Duck, what's the matter with you? Your uncle Danny wouldn't have missed that one!" And everyone who heard him would laugh. Everyone but me.

When the day of the team practice came around, Mr. Schneider picked us up and deposited us at the Station Hill ball field. My brother, Pat, wasn't on the team, since he was only in the second grade, but he came along to watch the practice and see his friends. He had a lot of friends. For some mysterious reason everyone seemed to like him.

The town baseball field had a backstop and real bases. Miss Scott was there to greet us, but she left to supervise the girls' volleyball team practice over at the school.

Henry Adamson was at the controls for our practice, and he'd brought along a slugger from the town team to exercise the outfield. I was assigned to play left field. Axel was playing center field, next to me, and as usual, he got most of the action. He was a ball hog, and he was faster than I was. Sometimes the ball would be coming down between us—sometimes it was even way over on my side—and Axel would shout "I got it," and he'd be under it before I got there. He acted as if half the outfield belonged to him.

Axel had been playing baseball for three years, and he thought he was superior to me. I guess he was. He seldom missed any catch he went for, so no one ever objected to him hogging the field except for me. I didn't keep my irritation about it to myself, not that it did much good.

Ernie Hawreluk over in right field suffered worse than I did. He did get to back up Vincent Slade on first base, but as far as outfield flies went, Axel took everything he could get to. Unlike me, Ernie never complained about it. Instead of calling Ernie by his proper name, Axel called him Harelip, just because he had a little lisp. Ernie never complained about that either.

After the practice was finished, we hiked over to the school to meet the buses. When we got there, Miss Scott told us that we needed a name for our team, and so after some debate, we named ourselves the Eagles. She laughed and informed us that the Melody team had called themselves the Hawks. So as far as names went, we had them beat.

The news about the big game between the two schools had spread quickly because baseball was very popular. Every town of any size had a baseball field, and many of them had teams made up of men from the local area. Station Hill's team—the Sodbusters—were currently the county champions.

While the original idea was to have a small, friendly, midsummer get-together between our two schools, by the time the great day arrived, the baseball game had become a do-or-die contest for town superiority, and the passions it unleashed among the general population easily equaled those that engulfed the North and South on the eve of the Civil War.

On the big day the buses deposited everybody at the Station Hill School. The kids automatically assembled into two camps—Melodies with Melodies and Station Hillers with Station Hillers—and it stayed that way throughout lunch despite all attempts by our teachers to get us to mix. As soon as lunch was over, the baseball teams set out on foot for the town field.

Most of the townspeople from Station Hill and Melody, along with half the countryside, had gathered there to watch our friendly little baseball game. They had come in trucks and cars, and on foot. They had come with their little kids and their babies and their dogs, along with picnic lunches and bottles of pop. They surrounded the infield on both sides, lying in wait for us, and they let out a solid cheer when they saw us approaching.

Mother and Father were there, alongside Uncle Max and Aunt Margaret. Our dog, Bounce, was there too, running across the outfield in pursuit of two other dogs with confused bloodlines like his. Charlie Pears, our neighbor, had also driven in to watch us lambaste Melody School. He was sitting on the roof of his truck, basking in the sun like a giant toad. Everyone I knew was there, including the beautiful Catherine Schneider.

The game was all very pleasant and easygoing—at first. It was as if the gentle noon-hour scrub games at our two schools had simply been merged together. However, before the second inning was over, the crowd was shouting at us like a pack of frenzied banshees. Half of them encouraged the pitcher, while the other half urged the batter to knock the ball into outer space. Half the crowd moaned with disappointment at every little error, while the other half shrieked with joy at the same misplay. The tension built higher and higher, until it felt like we were engaged in an all-out contest for survival instead of a kids' ball game.

The pressure from the crowd made me nervous, but it also helped keep me alert and wary. I was absolutely determined to hold up my end and defeat the enemy from Melody.

The game went forward in a roughly even manner, with both teams making errors, both hitting and scoring about equally well. Unfortunately, my batting skills had deserted me. "I'm telling Uncle Danny on you," Axel Smart sneered at me on the way to the outfield. I'd struck out again, ending the inning with a man on third base.

I finally got a base hit in the seventh inning. It got me to second base, and I managed to score before the inning was over. I breathed a huge sigh of relief when I tramped on home plate. At last I'd managed to help us on our march toward victory. And I hadn't made any errors either. Actually, I hardly had a chance to make an error because Axel was constantly running into my area and catching flies that should have been mine.

At the top of the ninth inning with two out, the score was eleven to nine in our favor. We were so close to victory, we could almost taste it. However, there were two Melody players on base—one on first and one on second—when a guy they called Big Murray came out of the Melody pack and picked up the bat. Axel, Ernie, and I all backed up. The last time Big Murray was at bat, he'd hit a long fly into the far reaches of left field. It was a catch I had desperately wanted to make, and it should have been mine, but Axel had shouldered me aside and taken it from me.

While Big Murray was loosening up and trying out the bat I saw my mother in the crowd. "Go, Donald! Go!" she called to me. My father cupped his hands about his mouth and added his vocal cords to the symphony of cheers while Pat and his friends watched expectantly from the edge of the field.

Big Murray stationed himself beside the plate and bent forward slightly. He drew the bat back and looked menacingly at the pitcher. The first pitch was low, but he swung hard at it anyway, and he hit it. It was a glancing blow, and the result was a pop fly headed a bit beyond the infield. It was a left field ball, and my instincts were good. I was off in the right direction as soon as I heard the crack of the bat, and I'd covered half the distance to the infield before the ball reached the top of its trajectory. I knew I could get to it in plenty of time. And this one was all mine.

The ball was on the way down and I was running flat out, when Axel's shoulder brushed against me.

"I got it!" he cried.

"It's mine!" I yelled.

I then deliberately shouldered Axel aside. He deserved it. He was definitely invading my territory again. But unfortunately, when I bumped him away, he tripped and tumbled to the ground, and for just an instant, I took my eye off the ball. The ball then completed its trajectory, smacking into my forehead. Darkness fell, then little silver stars popped out of the black sky and swirled around in front of my eyes. While I was on the ground, knocked out cold, Axel managed to pick up the ball and throw it in. But it was too late. By the time Henry had it in hand, Big Murray had touched home plate. A home run on a pop fly.

But at that moment I didn't know any of this. When I came to, I had no idea where I was. I somehow managed to get to my feet and staggered toward Miss Scott, who was striding across the diamond to meet me. Henry got to me at the same time, and together they brought me in.

Most of the crowd watched silently as I was led off the field. There were a few catcalls, but I was too dazed to realize they were directed at me. When we reached the sidelines, I collapsed. My father picked me up, and we followed old Doctor Thorne and his wife across the street and into their house, which also served as the town clinic.

"Is he going to die?" Pat asked.

"Don't be silly," someone said.

The doctor led us into his office, and my father lifted me onto the examination table. I sat there staring into space like a struck duck until the doctor waved a finger in front of my face.

"Follow my finger with your eyes," he said quietly.

He listened to my heart with his stethoscope and asked me some questions, including my name. It took me a second or two, but I finally came up with it.

"Donald Duck," I said.

"He's had a mild concussion," the doctor said at the end of it all. "Put him to bed, but wake him up every couple of hours and check that he's alert and his pupils are the same size. If in doubt, bring him back to see me."

As soon as I stepped down from the table, I started to throw up. A split second later old Mrs. Thorne was holding a large, two-eared metal pot under my chin. While I was retching into her pot she said it would make me feel better. It didn't. I still felt like I'd been hit on the head with the blunt end of an ax.

On the way out, I began to feel strange—as though I was only half there. I had no memory of the game at all. In fact, I had very little memory of anything. Father kept his hand on my back and guided me across the street to the truck. In a brief, shimmering moment of clarity, I saw a cluster of people staring at us.

"You'll feel better when we get home," Mother promised me as we drove out of town. When we got home, they looked into my eyes like the doctor had done.

As soon as my brain began to function properly, a ghastly beast that had been lurking somewhere in the depths of my memory stood up on its hideous hind legs and staggered forward to confront me.

"I missed it!" I cried out.

"It doesn't matter," Father assured me. "It could have happened to anyone."

But it hadn't happened to anyone. It had happened to me.

"Who won?" I cried out.

"Melody won," Pat said.

My stomach went hollow. My heart lurched sideways.

My breathing stopped. I had missed the catch that would have brought victory to our school. I had missed the catch that would have covered me in glory. Instead, I'd covered myself with shame. Forever and ever, I would carry the stain of my failure wherever I went. Forever and ever, misery and regret would be my constant companions. I had single-handedly lost the big game.

I turned my head and looked out the window. I wanted to cry, but tears were useless. Nothing could change what had happened. There was nothing I could do. Nothing. A few moments later Mother put me and my colossal headache to bed and tucked us in. I was soon lost in a troubled, aching sleep.

CHAPTER TWO
Ruined

"You look funny," Pat informed me as I crawled out of bed the next morning.

He was right. When I looked in the mirror, I was astonished by the monster staring back at me. On the left side of my forehead, about an inch above my eyebrow, I had a lump that was almost as big as the baseball that had caused it.

Below the lump I had a black eye, but that didn't bother me so much. It was the lump. It frightened me. The size of it. Mother must have agreed with me because when she saw it, she ran to the door and rang the bell to summon my father. A moment later he calmly examined the mountainous bulge protruding from my forehead.

"How do you feel?" he asked me. "Have you got a headache?"

"No," I said.

Despite my objections they took me into town to see Doctor Thorne again. He was gone, but Mrs. Thorne was there. I could tell from the look on her face that she was also amazed by the size of my bump.

"Take him home and put him to bed," she said. "I'll send the doctor out to you as soon as he gets back."

We saw people going into the church as we headed out of town. It was Sunday. I hadn't realized it until then.

"Are we going to church today?" Pat asked.

"No, not today," Mother said.

"Are we going to Annie's?" he asked. Annie was our cousin. She lived on a nearby farm with my uncle Max and aunt Margaret.

"No. We'll just have a nice quiet day by ourselves," she said.

"Is he going to die?" Pat asked.

"Of course not," Mother said reassuringly, stroking my cheek. "He's just got a little bump on his forehead, that's all."

For the rest of the way home, Pat stared at the humongous lump on my forehead while I kept wondering if it was going to kill me.

As soon as we got home, I went back to the mirror and looked again at the monster from another planet— the one with the little head growing out of the big one. It was still as big as before, so I went upstairs and lay down on the bed. As soon as I closed my eyes, I saw the ball coming at me again.

It occurred to me that if the lump killed me, I wouldn't have to see any of the kids at school ever again. But I was afraid of dying. I was afraid I'd go to hell because I was not such a nice person. Even if I somehow managed to get into heaven, I'd be stuck somewhere down at the far end of the bottom row, alongside the other doubtful angels.

The doctor came and went, then compresses soaked in our cold well water also came and went, endlessly. Miraculously, the huge bump had pretty well disappeared after just one day of this simple treatment. Exactly where it went, I didn't know, but good riddance to it. But I still had a stupendous black eye to remind me of my humiliation.

The morning I was allowed outside, I ran into my father on my way into the barn. He looked at me and smiled.

"Nice shiner," he said.

"Yeah," I said.

"How's the head?"

"It's okay."

"No headache?"

"No," I said.

I looked up at him, and my eyes filled with tears. I couldn't stop them.

"I know how you're feeling," he said, looking down at me. "But it wasn't your fault. That guy was crowding you."

"The ball bounced off my head and I lost the game," I said. "Everyone will think I'm a fool."

"A few of them might tease you a little, but it was just an accident. In a little while, they'll have forgotten about it," he said with a parting pat on my shoulder.

He was trying to make me feel better, but it didn't work. Nothing would ever make me feel better. I climbed up to the loft and lay down in the hay. But as soon as I closed my eyes, it was there again.

The ball coming toward me . . .

I went over to the loft doors and looked down at the corral. There was a coil of old hemp rope on the floor beside me. One end of it was fastened to a crossbeam above my head. I climbed down the rope and walked directly past Rodger. He was a mean old bull and he didn't like me, but I didn't care whether he charged me or not. In fact, a few months in the hospital might be just what I needed. But Rodger was so surprised by my sudden appearance that he forgot to try to kill me.

A few minutes later I was walking along the creek. The sun was still warm, the air still fresh, and the water was still cool and clear, but I didn't care about any of it.

If I'd simply missed the fly, then it would have been just plain disappointment over losing the game. Sure, some people would blame me, but the whole thing would have been over and forgotten in a few days. But having the ball bounce off my dome! Oh Lord! That changed everything. It changed it from a simple disappointment to a comic moment that everyone would remember for the rest of their lives. It made me a clown and a fool. I could already hear Axel crowing, "Hey, Donald Duck. Have you told your famous uncle Danny how you lost the game for us? Huh? Have you told him how you tried to catch the ball with your head? Huh? Huh?"

How I longed to forget that hideous moment out in left field. I was worn out from thinking about it. But nothing in the world was strong enough to take my mind off it. Or so I thought.

CHAPTER THREE
Robin Hood

A few days after my humiliation, I heard Mother and Father talking about me in the living room. I stopped halfway down the stairs and listened.

"He's so terribly depressed," Mother said.

"He'll get over it," he replied.

"But I've never seen him like this before," she said. "He's always so full of energy. It's like he's gone into hibernation."

"Relax and enjoy it while you can," he said.

"I can't relax. I'm worried about him," she said.

"I'll tell you what. We'll take him to a movie. That'll cheer him up," Father said.

And so, in the hope that it might cure my hibernation and depression, we went to the city to see a movie. The movie was about Robin Hood, and I loved every moment of it. While I was watching it I forgot about all my troubles, but as soon as it was over, I was back in my dismal old world, back to a life of humiliation and regret.

Lying in bed that night, with the moonlight creeping along the wall, with Pat fast asleep beside me, I thought about Robin Hood, about how he leaped from pillar to post like a jungle cat when he was trapped in the banquet hall. I remembered how fast and sure he was as he moved silently through the forest. I thought about how deadly he was with his bow and arrows. And then an idea came to me—an idea that quickly put on weight and spread throughout my brain until it pushed away the gloomy memories of that dreadful day on the ball field.

I would become an expert archer, like Robin Hood. No one would be able to match me at shooting arrows. That wouldn't be too hard to do. No one else I knew had a bow and arrows. Of course, I didn't intend to rob the rich and give to the poor like Robin Hood did. That was against the law in Montana, and out here the law could see you coming and going from twenty miles away. Out here the law had cars and I had nothing, not even a bicycle. And besides, there were no rich people to rob around here. Mr. Schneider was the closest thing we had to it, but he had five daughters and two dogs to support.

After I'd learned how to shoot arrows like Robin Hood, I would show Rachel and a few others how lethal I'd become. They would tell other others, and soon I would become known all over the countryside as the Deadly Archer. Then everyone would respect me, and no one would care about a little thing like missing a stupid catch.

Self-improvement. It's what life is all about, I thought.

Of course, in order to become the Deadly Archer, I needed a bow and arrow set. And I needed it right away, before school started. So the next morning I ran downstairs and found Mother alone in the kitchen. I looked at her with pleading eyes—one of them surrounded by a large black-and-yellow circle—and I asked her if she would buy me a bow and arrow set. She looked back at me in a way that was partly sympathetic and partly unsympathetic. Unfortunately, the unsympathetic part won out.

"Don't be silly," she said. "We can't afford that kind of thing. Anyway, those things are dangerous."

"But Mom..."

"The answer is no," she said. "And I'm not going to change my mind, so don't ask me again."

Although I didn't think my chances were very great, I ran outside to look for my father. I found him underneath the combine, poking around in its underbelly.

"Dad?"

"Yeah?"

"Would you buy me a bow and arrow set?"

"What for?"

"To shoot with," I said. "Like Robin Hood."

"Sorry. We can't afford things like that right now," he

grunted. "They say electricity is coming next year, so we're going to need every penny we can scrape up."

I wandered down past the corral where Rodger was nibbling at a tuft of grass over in the corner. He snorted at me, challenging me to climb over the fence and give him another chance to kill me. But I didn't care about what Rodger wanted. I didn't care about anything. My father's words had dashed all my hopes and thrown me back into the pit of despair.

However, I could not be kept down for long. Later, while I was sitting with Bounce on the bank of our little creek, I made a sacred vow that I would not rest until I had an archery set and had learned to use it with deadly accuracy.

On Saturday, Mother drove Pat and me to the little city of Wistola, as usual. We helped her unload Maggie— our one-ton truck—carrying her vegetables and eggs to her stall in the market garden. As soon as that was done, I took off to search through the stores. I found exactly what I was looking for at Plate's Hardware and Sporting Goods—a beautiful archery set for just eight dollars and ninety-nine cents. I immediately ran back to the stall and told her about my discovery.

"How many times do I have to tell you? We can't afford that kind of thing!" she said. "Now stop talking about it, or you're going to drive me nuts!"

"You could make one from a branch," Pat said.

"Mind your own business!" I screamed at him.

"Don't shout around here!" Mother shouted at me.

After we got home, I wandered out along the creek

and sat down at the edge of the beaver pond. I felt about as low as I'd ever felt in my life. I might have drowned myself, but the water wasn't deep enough.

When I got back to the house, Mother was busy making doughnuts. Her hair was straggling down over her forehead, and she was sweating from the oily heat. Pat was at the table, munching on a doughnut.

"Can I have an extra one to feed the ducks with," he asked her.

"My doughnuts are not for feeding ducks," she said.

She gave me a doughnut, and I held it up and looked through the hole at her.

"This would make a good target if I had a bow and arrow to shoot at it," I said.

"Stop it, Donald. You're not getting that archery set. You'll just have to find something else to do for the rest of your vacation."

The rest of my summer vacation only amounted to a few measly weeks. How I dreaded the day I would have to return to school. It was coming on fast, and it looked like there would not be a lethal archer facing the jeering crowd. Not unless I got that one essential piece of equipment, and got it soon.

I went into our little woods and pretended it was Sherwood Forest. Pat was wandering around in there too, looking at birds. I imagined he was the sheriff of Nottingham, and I shot him four times with my imaginary bow and arrows, but he didn't seem to notice all the arrows sticking out of him.

"Why are you wasting your time watching birds?" I said roughly. "They're all the same. Two wings and two feet and a bunch of feathers."

"They're interesting," he protested.

"When I get my archery set, I'm going to kill them all," I promised him.

At suppertime Pat complained to Mother about my threat, but she only smiled.

"Don't worry about it," she said. "He'll never get one."

"Yes I will!" I said hotly. "I'm saving up for it."

"Don't shout in the kitchen," she shouted.

"How much have you saved so far?" Father calmly asked me.

"Forty-four cents," I replied glumly.

"Well, it's a start," he said.

"I'm saving every penny I get," I vowed.

"No more movies, then?" Mother asked with a sly smile. She was right. I couldn't give up my Saturday movies. They were the only good thing left in my life.

"Except for movies," I admitted.

They both laughed, and I knew they were thinking that I would never save enough money to buy it.

Later on, while I was lying on the bed thinking about my desperate situation, the door opened and Father came in. He opened his wallet, took out a dusty dollar bill, and handed it to me. "Here's a little help toward your archery set," he said.

"Thanks, Dad!"

With his generous contribution to the fund, hope

returned in full force, and it was right then that I had a brilliant idea. "If I collected a whole bunch of extra beer bottles for my archery set, would you take them to town in the truck?"

"Yeah, but not in dribs and drabs," he said. "You'd have to get enough together to make the trip worthwhile."

"I'll collect enough to buy the archery set!" I exclaimed enthusiastically. "Then we can take them all in at once, and I'll get it the same day."

"Sure," he said with a laugh. "That'll be fine. But in the meantime, do me a favor."

"What?"

"Stop yakking about that archery set when your mother's around. In fact, don't even mention it to her."

"I won't," I promised.

He stopped at the door and smiled at me.

"You know, kiddo, it's going to take an awful lot of bottles to get that much money. I reckon you'll just about be old enough to go to college by the time you've got it."

He left the room chuckling to himself.

I was chuckling, too, because I knew where there was a huge supply of beer bottles just waiting for me to pick them up. Thousands and thousands of them were scattered over the pasture by Charlie Pears's old house.

Charlie was our neighbor up on the hill, and last year he'd given Pat and me free rein to help ourselves to his crop of beer bottles. Ever since then, we'd been collecting enough to pay for our Saturday movie when we went to town with Mother. Father knew all this, of course.

What he didn't know was how many beer bottles were still left up there. He was in for a big surprise when he found out.

I found a pencil and sat down to figure out how many bottles I'd need in order to get my archery set.

My cousin Annie was dead right when she said mathematics was an evil invented by Satan for teachers to torture kids with. However, after a lot of deep thought, I was finally able to come up with the answer I needed. To begin with, since the archery set cost eight dollars and ninety-nine cents, I calculated that in addition to the dollar and forty-four cents I had, I needed another seven dollars and fifty-five cents. Beer bottles sold for ten cents a case, so I divided it out and discovered that I would need seventy-five and one-half cases to get that much money. Since there were twelve beer bottles in a case, that worked out to a total of nine hundred and six bottles.

Oh happiness! Collecting nine hundred and six bottles would be no problem at all! All I had to do was gather them up at Charlie's and bring them down the hill for Father to haul into Wistola for me. I'd work night and day, and before you could say Jack Robinson, I'd be shooting arrows all over the place.

I found Pat up in the loft in the barn, sitting between the open doors with his legs dangling over the edge. He was watching some early Canada geese that had come down at the edge of the nearest wheat field. I sat down beside him and stretched my dollar out in front of his eyes.

"Where'd you get it?" he exclaimed.

"Dad gave it to me," I said. "Now I only need to collect nine hundred and six beer bottles, then I can buy my archery set."

"You aren't going to shoot geese with it?" he asked with sudden alarm.

"I might," I said. "Once I get good enough."

I left him contemplating this horrendous idea and ran down the road to see Rachel. Pat and I used a couple of gunnysacks to carry our weekly bottle harvest down from Charlie's, but this project was too big for that. I needed a wagon, and I'd seen an old Radio Flyer down at the Schneiders', hiding in the grass behind a shed.

Catherine—Rachel's oldest sister—opened the door. Her golden hair was spread across her shoulders, and the stars in her eyes glittered down at me.

"Oh, you poor kid," Catherine said. "Does it still hurt?"

She was talking about my black eye. I shook my head at her.

She smiled and gently touched my head, and I felt as if I were looking at the divine face of Ozma of Oz. Suddenly everything seemed to be happening in slow motion.

"Rachel's gone to town with Dad and Mom," she said. "They've all gone, except me."

I swallowed with difficulty and tried to say something, but I couldn't speak. Her glittering eyes had paralyzed my tongue. I forced myself to look away from them and managed to get a few words out.

"I need to borrow your wagon," I said.

"What wagon?"

"Your little red wagon. It's behind the shed."

"Oh, sure. Go ahead," she said.

I pulled the wagon out of the tall grass and discovered that it was still in working order. Catherine came to the door again as I went by.

"What are you going to do with it?" she asked me.

"I need to haul nine hundred and six beer bottles down from Charlie's," I said.

For some reason she thought this was funny, and her laughter made my heart beat faster. I waited until she stopped so I could explain myself.

"I'm going to buy a bow and arrow set," I informed her. "Like Robin Hood's."

"Well, good luck," she said.

When I got home, Pat was still up in the loft spying on the geese.

"I borrowed a wagon from the Schneiders'," I said. "Let's go!"

"Go where?" he asked.

"To haul bottles down from Charlie's. I just told you. We have to get nine hundred and six of them so I'll be able to buy my archery set. Come on, let's go!"

"I'm not going," he said. "I want to watch the geese."

"If you help me, I'll let you shoot it," I promised.

"No, I'm watching the geese," he said.

"You've been watching those stupid geese all morning. Come on."

"They're not stupid."

"All right, then. They're smarter than they look. Come on."

"No, I don't want to."

"Okay, I won't shoot any geese with it," I promised him.

My promise didn't work. It was clear that he no longer trusted me. I used every trick in the book, I even said something nice about geese, but I couldn't budge him. Once he'd made up his mind, he was unbudgeable.

"You'll be sorry!" I screamed. "I'm going to hunt down those geese as soon as I get my archery set! I'll kill them all!"

I found an apple crate by the kindling pile, and it fit into the wagon like it had been specially made for it. With this box in place, the number of bottles I could carry would be doubled at least.

A few minutes later I was pulling the wagon up the hill, wondering how long it would take to haul nine hundred and six beer bottles down. I figured it wouldn't be too hard to do, since it was pretty well downhill all the way, as far as moving the bottles went. The wagon would be empty going back up, so that part of the trip would be easy and quick too.

When I reached Charlie's, I headed for the pasture opposite the window. The barbed-wire fence had fallen over in the middle of the area, which would make it easy to move the wagon in and out.

Seconds later I was standing in the midst of one of

the world's great treasures. All around me the ground was littered with multitudes of brown beer bottles. Some of them were broken, but the broken glass posed no danger to me, since my boots had thick, hard soles. I did think it was a great waste, all those broken bottles, but I never mentioned it to Charlie. I didn't want to make him mad at me.

While I loaded the wagon I marveled again at how good Charlie was at throwing beer bottles through his window. They were spread all over the pasture, a considerable distance past the fence line. He couldn't throw them out of the window in the winter, of course. In the winter the window was closed and frozen shut, so he had to step outside the back door and throw them from his porch. There were fewer bottles broken in the winter than in the summer because the snow cushioned them.

I worked hard, and it wasn't long before the apple crate was full. I jammed two more in between the back of the box and the end of the wagon, then I headed out with my first load. In all my excitement I had neglected to count the bottles as I loaded them on board. However, I reckoned there must be at least two dozen beer bottles in there. Maybe as many as three dozen. No, not that many. About two dozen.

It's a lot easier hauling them down in the wagon than with sacks, I thought as I pulled my load out of the pasture. What's more, I didn't have to worry about breaking them like I did when I carried them down in a sack.

I wondered if the Schneiders would give me the wagon.

They didn't seem to use it anymore. If they ever needed it for something, I'd be happy to let them borrow it back—provided I wasn't using it myself.

As I headed toward the road I tried to figure out how many trips up and down the hill I'd have to make. I knew that I needed seventy-five cases. If I hauled two dozen bottles down on each trip, that would be two cases per trip. So how many trips would I have to make? How many?

By the time I'd reached the edge of the hill, I'd discovered that I was not able to do arithmetic in my head, not even something as simple as that, not even when I was interested in the outcome. But although I didn't know the final answer for sure, it seemed to me that there was going to be half a trip left over in the end, and that puzzled me. How could I make half a trip?

I wondered who invented fractions, and why they did it. Why didn't they just round things off?

I was walking backward down the hill, holding the wagon back with the handle, thinking about the half-a-trip problem, when suddenly the handle went up in the air and the wagon came after me. I leaped sideways, still holding on to the handle, and it overturned. Two dozen beer bottles—or thereabouts—went rolling down the hill.

One of the bottles was smashed during the overturning, so I picked up all the pieces and put them in the bottom of the wagon. I didn't want anyone, especially us or Charlie, to get a flat tire.

Most of the bottles had wound up in the ditch alongside the road. I quickly gathered them up and started down the hill with them. This time I let the wagon go backward, ahead of me, so that it was pulling on my arms and couldn't run over me. It worked better, and I made it safely down to the bottom. However, it was a lot slower than I wanted it to be.

When I came into our yard with the load, I heard the bell ringing. Then Pat came running toward me.

"Supper's ready!" he shouted.

After supper Father and I went outside, and I showed him my first load.

"I borrowed the wagon from the Schneiders'," I informed him.

"Not a bad haul for half a day's work," he commented. "At this rate you should have enough in a year or two," he added with a laugh.

"Where should I put them?"

"Put them over there behind those bushes," he said, pointing at some lilac bushes just off the lane. "When you get enough to make it worthwhile, we'll take them into town."

After he'd left, I emptied the wagon, laying the bottles in a row behind the bushes. I discovered that I was two bottles short of two dozen, and I resolved to count them in the future in order to bring down an even two dozen every trip.

After supper, just as I was starting up the hill, I heard a shout from Rachel. She ran to catch up with me.

"What are you doing with our old wagon?" she asked.

"I'm collecting beer bottles at Charlie's. I need to haul

nine hundred and six of them down to our place so I can buy an archery set," I said as we continued up the hill.

"What's an archery set?" she asked.

"It's a set of bow and arrows," I said. "Like Robin Hood had in Sherwood Forest."

"Nine hundred and six?" she asked with a puzzled frown.

"Yeah. Nine hundred and six."

"That's a lot of beer bottles," she observed. "Has he got that many?"

"He's got millions of them," I assured her.

"Father drinks beer," she said. "He makes it in the basement."

"I can bring down twenty-four at a time," I said.

"It's going to take a long time," she observed.

"I'm going to become a lethal archer," I informed her.

"What's that?"

"I'll show you when the time comes," I promised her.

"Wanda fell off the roof this morning," she said. "She wasn't killed though, because she landed on the roof of the car. Now there's a big dent in it. On its roof. Daddy yelled when he saw it. But he was kinda glad about it, too, because it saved her life. Afterward he had a bad headache."

"Did the doctor come out?"

"Oh no. She wasn't even hurt. Do you want to see the dent in our car? It's a big one."

"Yeah, but not now. I'm too busy," I said.

"She thought there was a new batch of swallows in

the eave around back, Wanda did. That's why she went up there. She stepped on the water barrel and climbed up the downspout. She's very athletic. Last year she climbed right up to the top of our elm tree, and she..."

And on and on Rachel went, telling me various Wanda things about which I had no interest.

"Do you want to help me load the bottles into the wagon?" I asked her when we reached the top of the hill.

"I can't. Father said we can't go to Charlie's."

"Why not?"

"I don't know."

She turned and headed back down the hill as I pulled the wagon into Charlie's place. As soon as I'd crossed the fallen-down fence into the pasture, I set to work. A little while later, I had another load on board and I was once again on my way home.

I noticed again how slow it was going down the hill backward—with the wagon going backward, that is. I tried to think of how I could make it go down the other way without the risk of spilling the load, but no ideas came to me.

After I'd unloaded the bottles behind the bushes, I ran to the house to figure out how many trips I'd have to make. I opened a clean page in my arithmetic scribbler and forced my mind into its highest gear.

I needed seventy-five and one-half cases, total, and I brought down two cases on each trip, so I divided two into seventy-five and one-half. After some difficulty, I discovered the answer was thirty-seven and three-quarters.

In other words, I would have to make thirty-seven and three-quarters trips up to Charlie's. I couldn't understand where the three-quarters of a trip came from, nor why I should be making three-quarters of a trip at all. What use would that be? It hurt my brain to think about it, so I rounded the fraction off by letting the total number of trips be thirty-eight.

A few minutes later, I pulled the wagon out of our yard and started back up the hill. Only thirty-six more trips to go. I was still hopeful, but the whole thing was taking much longer than I'd expected.

"Rome wasn't built in a day," my father often said. That may have been true, but he also said, "All roads lead to Rome," and that wasn't true. Our road didn't. It didn't lead anywhere in particular. It just led to Charlie's in one direction and the Schneiders' in the other, and then to some other roads.

It was beginning to get dark when I unloaded the wagon for the third time, so I quit for the day. It was a good start. I'd managed to bring down a total of three loads—six cases in all.

I'll do a lot better tomorrow, I thought.

CHAPTER FOUR
Obstacles

The next morning while Pat and I were busy shoveling down our porridge, Mother announced that she was going to Wistola to see Rita. Rita was her best friend. She was also my best friend's mother.

"You can go swimming with Milton," she said.

"Can I go swimming too?" Pat asked her.

"If you remember to bring your bathing suit," she said.

"I'm not going," I said. Mother looked at me as though she couldn't believe her ears. I'd never before voluntarily missed the chance to go into Wistola. We'd lived there during the war, before Father came home and moved us out to the farm.

"What?"

"I'm going to collect bottles," I explained.

She gave me a strange look, as though I might be an unnatural substitute for her real son.

"Suit yourself," she said with a frown.

The truck went out of the yard and turned right. I followed it out and turned left. A few seconds later I was plodding up the hill with my wagon.

When I returned with the first load, Father called me over.

"The pigpen needs to be cleaned," he said.

Just the thought of it made me groan inside. A few minutes later I followed him and the wheelbarrow and the scoop shovels over to the horrible, stinking little building. The smell was almost enough to make me throw up.

"I slept in a pigsty once," he said as we shoveled the manure into the wheelbarrow. He laughed at the memory of it. "It was during the Depression, before I'd met your mother. We were wandering along a country road some-where, me and my friend Joe Cantilla. We were looking for work. We'd been roaming around for days, and we hardly knew where we were. We were half-starved—and cold. Boy were we cold!

"There was nothing anywhere, and we walked and walked, on and on, until we were just too beat to go any farther. By this time it was dark. We tried to sleep in a ditch, but we nearly froze to death, so we had to get up and keep going. Then just before dawn, we came across a farm. It was too early to wake the people up, so we looked around for a place to warm up. Their barn had burned down, so it was either the chicken coop or the pigpen. The pigpen would be the warmest inside, and that's all we cared about. To get warm. So we bedded down in there. And that's where the farmer found us in the morning, sleeping alongside his pigs.

"We were afraid he'd be mad, but he laughed at us. Laughed and laughed. And we laughed too, even though we didn't personally think it was all that funny. But we were hoping he'd feed us, so we went along with it. Anyway, he did feed us, but he made us eat out in the pasture because we stunk so bad. Oatmeal porridge and black bread was what he gave us, and it was the best thing I ever ate in my life, before or since. Then he sent us on our way with a couple of boiled eggs and some more bread. When it warmed up in the afternoon, we had a swim in a slough with our clothes on and that eased our smell a bit."

"Did you ever find some work?" I asked.

"Later on, we came to a little town and it had a bowling alley, so we went in and asked if he needed any help to set pins or anything. But no one was bowling. After a while, he offered us a job waxing and polishing the bowling alleys. We worked all day, and when we were finished, he gave us two bits for the day's work. A quarter between us for all that hard work. We bought some bags of peanuts with it, and that's all we had to eat until we got back home. Two and a half little bags of peanuts each."

He had a faraway expression in his eyes.

"I remember it like it was yesterday," he said.

Three hours later when we'd finished cleaning out the pigpen, we took turns having a bath in our old galvanized tub, next to the kitchen stove. After our late lunch was over, I had just enough energy left to make two trips up and down the hill.

"I didn't go swimming," Pat informed me when they got home. "I went to a movie with Milton instead."

"Congratulations," I said, my voice dripping with acid.

"It was *Tarzan and the Leopard Woman*," he announced with a smug smile. "And there was a cowboy one with Roy Rogers."

I moaned inside. I didn't care at all about missing Roy Rogers, but Tarzan movies were my favorite.

I fell asleep after supper, and when I woke up, it was already dark outside. It was too late to make any more bottle trips, but I vowed to make six trips the next day, even if it killed me.

I woke up in the middle of the night. While I lay awake thinking of Father's story, I began to hear whispers coming through the register. I got down on my hands and knees and listened.

"Tell me about it in the morning," he said in a sleepy voice.

"I'm telling you about it now," she said. "I dreamed he shot himself with it."

"You can't shoot yourself with your own bow and arrow. It's impossible," he muttered. "Go to sleep."

"I know. But it wasn't just that. It was the feeling. It was a bad feeling."

"It was just a dream," he said. "Go back to sleep. You'll feel better in the morning."

Her next words made my heart stand still: "I don't want him to get that archery set," she said.

"Well, you should have said so sooner," he replied. "It's too late now."

"Well, I'm saying it now. Those things are dangerous," she said.

"Shovels are dangerous," he said. "Remember?"

"I certainly do. That's what's bothering me," she said. "If they can almost kill themselves with a shovel, think of what they could do with a bow and arrow."

"The point is, things are only dangerous if they're misused, and I'll make sure he does it safely. If he ever gets one, I'll set up some straw bales for him to shoot at. It'll be perfectly safe."

"I still don't like it," she said.

"Look, it'll be years before he's saved enough money, and he'll have forgotten all about it by then. So stop worrying and go to sleep."

"You don't know him as well as I do. I've seen that look in his eyes before. When he wants something—"

"Wanting is not getting," Father interrupted.

"You shouldn't have agreed to help him."

"I only said I'd take his bottles in when he has a good load. It'll take him months to get enough together for a load, and we'll be buried in snow long before then. So stop worrying and go to sleep."

"I still have a bad feeling," she said.

"I do too. Mine's from a lack of sleep," he said with a sigh.

The conversation frightened me. I had to get a move on and get the load of bottles down before she convinced him to stop me from getting my archery set. *Ten loads tomorrow even if it kills me,* I promised myself.

The next morning when I arrived on the scene with the wagon, Charlie was sitting with his feet over the end of the porch with a bottle of beer in his hand. His orange cat was in his lap.

"Pow! Right in the noggin," he said. "Didn't you see it comin'?"

"I would have got it if Axel hadn't pushed me," I protested. That wasn't exactly the truth, but sometimes the exact truth is too complicated to explain.

"Whatcha need all the bottles for?" he asked me.

"I'm going to buy a bow and arrow set," I informed him. I then took time out to explain everything.

"Yeah, I heard about this Robin Hood guy," he muttered when I'd finished the story. "Never thought much of them bows and arrows though. Guns is better. Just ask the Injuns." He then got up and went into the house, leaving me alone to think about his opinion.

I had just started to load the wagon when he came back out. "Come 'ere!" he shouted.

He stepped down from the porch with his beautiful double-barreled shotgun in one hand and a big bagful of shells in the other. When he waved at me to follow him, I put one more bottle into the wagon and followed him into the adjacent pasture—into another sea of bottles. These were the ones he'd thrown from his back porch in the wintertime.

"We're gonna shoot some bottles," he said with a chuckle. "Pick one up."

All I wanted in life was to be left alone to collect my bottles without any distractions. But God was against me.

I picked up a beer bottle and looked at him.

"Throw it up in the air. Over there," he said, pointing with the shotgun.

I threw the bottle up in the air, but he shook his head.

"No, no. Not like that," he said with a frown. "Like this." He demonstrated by throwing a bottle high into the sky and then blasting it to smithereens with the shotgun.

I threw a bottle up as high as I could, and he fired at it when it reached the highest point in its trip upward. Just like the first one, the bottle shattered into a million fragments.

"Another one," he ordered cheerfully.

I threw the next one up and it suffered the same fate as the first two.

He never seemed to miss. But while it was interesting to see the bottles burst in the air, I hated to have to participate in the destruction of perfectly good beer bottles—especially since they were mine.

"Throw another one," he said.

I threw another one, and another and another, and I kept on throwing them each time he nodded at me to let one go. I had become a human catapult. All the same, I never thought of refusing him. Not only was he the sole source of my wealth, he was the kind of person you couldn't say no to.

"You're a good thrower," he said at one point as the destruction proceeded.

After he'd obliterated a couple of cases of my precious bottles, he loaded the shotgun again and handed it to me.

"Okay," he said. "Your turn."

He coached me on how to aim and fire at a flying bottle, and thus maximize my chances of destroying a little bit more of my wealth.

I had fired the shotgun once and I knew about its powerful recoil, so I fully expected it to knock me on my rear end. However, it didn't. The kick was powerful, but—much to my amazement—I withstood it. I didn't destroy a bottle with my first few shots, but I did kill one very effectively on my fourth try.

I spent half the morning out there with Charlie, either throwing bottles in the air or shooting at them. By the time it was over, I was pretty much hooked on the sport. After he'd gone inside, I walked back to the adjacent pasture and went back to work.

In the meantime, Charlie came back outside. He sat down on the end of the porch and watched me collect the bottles.

When I reached the fence on my way out, he stood up.

"Here's another one!" he yelled, throwing his latest empty bottle into the pasture behind me. Thinking it was the polite thing to do, I ran back and picked it up. I put it in the back of the wagon on top of the others.

Pat was waiting for me at the bottom of the hill.

"It's lunchtime," he said. "Who's shooting?"

"Charlie," I said. And that's all I said. If I'd told him I'd been shooting at bottles with Charlie, everyone would know about it before lunch was over and my instincts told me Mother wouldn't like it.

There was still plenty of daytime left after lunch, but I didn't go out. I was dead tired. What's more, I had a very sore shoulder that I couldn't complain about. So I spent the afternoon out in the loft reading a book and resting up. After supper I was still so tired that I fell asleep on the sofa. When I awoke, it was dark outside. Another day lost!

I wandered outside to go to the outhouse. Pat was out there, sitting on the step. During the summer he had developed the strange habit of going outside to sit on the steps before bedtime, gazing at the stars until he was told to come in. He seemed to enjoy it. As for me, all I cared about was collecting beer bottles. "Only forty-two more cases to go," I said to myself that night before I fell asleep.

The next day they all went to town, including my father. I refused to go, even though it was Saturday and I would miss my movie. I had great expectations for the day as I trudged up the hill. Six cases? Eight cases? Who knows? Maybe even ten cases!

I pulled the wagon into the pasture, but before I got started, Charlie came out onto the porch and shouted at me. He was wearing his red plaid shirt. It was the newest and cleanest shirt he had—the one he always wore when he was going somewhere.

"Come 'ere!" he shouted.

A few minutes later we were driving down the road.

God is against me, I thought.

He wouldn't tell me where we were going, but after we'd gone about two miles, the pressure of holding the secret in became too much for him and he told me.

"I'm gettin' a new dog." He grinned. "A collie. We always had collie dogs. They's the best." He went on to tell me the history of all the collies he'd had from the time he was a little boy up until the last one. The last one—Greta was her name—had died over two years ago, but he hadn't been able to bring himself to replace her until now.

We arrived at a very nice-looking farm well stocked with collies. The one Charlie picked out from the pack was a particularly fine animal. The people who were selling her gave us a demonstration of her abilities, and she was, at a rough guess, about nine times as smart as our dog, Bounce. She was nearly full-grown and already had a name, but Charlie renamed her Suzy.

On the way back Suzy sat quietly between us. She was unperturbed by the smells inside the cab—not by the new ones that wafted by from time to time, nor by the old ones that seeped out of the upholstery.

Although I enjoyed the trip, it took up most of the day. In fact, I had just arrived at the brow of the hill with my first load of bottles when I saw our truck turn into our driveway down below. After I'd unloaded the wagon, I was about to start out again when Pat came running toward me. There was a look of wild excitement on his face, and he was waving a strange metal object in his hand.

"Mother sold dead grampa's big clock and they bought me a telescope!" he cried. "See? They bought me a map of the stars too, but it's in the house 'cause I don't want to get it dirty."

I didn't wait to hear anything else. I just made an all-out dash for the door. Could it be? Could it be? If they'd bought Pat a telescope and a map of the stars, they had to buy me something too. I fully expected it to be that beautiful archery set at Plate's. They knew where it was. They knew how much it cost. They knew how much I longed to have it.

But my hopes were soon trampled into the ground. They had bought me something, but it wasn't the archery set. They had bought me a book about how things work— things like airplanes and doorbells and other stuff we didn't have. How could I even begin to express my sense of outrage and hurt? I could hardly speak, I was so devastated by their odious trick. I had been betrayed by my own parents.

What's more, Pat hadn't even asked for a telescope. All he'd ever done was sit on the back steps and stare at the sky and tell the people who were tripping over him that stars are beautiful.

"What about my archery set?" I asked them, my voice ravaged with despair.

"We bought you that nice book," Mother said.

"But I wanted an archery set," I protested.

"With electricity coming next year, we can't afford to spend money on unnecessary things," Father responded. "Anyway, right now nine bucks is way out of our league."

"But you bought Pat a telescope!" I exclaimed.

"A telescope is a completely different thing," Father said calmly. "It's not a toy. It's educational. Like the book we bought you."

"And it didn't cost any nine dollars," Mother added.

"I'll let you look through my telescope," Pat said obligingly later on when I wandered back outside.

"I'm never going to look through it as long as I live," I replied with tears in my eyes.

I meandered along the creek for a long time, then went the rest of the way to the Old Hermit's place. The Old Hermit was a veteran from the First World War who'd spent most of the war getting lost in the Arabian desert with his friend Larry. He'd built his shack in the bush along our creek and settled in for the duration as a full-time professional hermit. He had a calming effect on me, and I visited him now and then when I needed some calming. After I got there, I had a biscuit and a cup of tea with him, and he began to tell me another story about his days in Arabia.

"Then there was the time me and Larry drank some bad water in one of them so-called oases out there in the Sahara, and we got so sick that our guide wanted to be paid in advance for burying us. Then while we was dying, he comes over and tells us there's this special pomegranate he has, which is the only thing that will save us because it's an antidote to this kind of bad water we'd just drunk. Then he holds it up for us to see.

"We're both lying there in the sand, dying fast, so this pomegranate is looking pretty good right then. Then he tells us what it'll cost us to buy it, so Larry raises his head a little and gives him a look of disbelief, like he's never heard of such an outrageous price for a pomegranate. He's dying and he can only whisper now, so he whispers, 'It'd be a lot cheaper to get buried.' And then the haggling begins. Arabs love to haggle, you know. To them it's half the fun of buying and selling. Anyway, Larry gets him all the way down to half price, which is the usual thing out there, and the deal is done.

"We all shake hands on it, though Larry and me can hardly lift our hands, and then our guide cuts the pome-granate in half and hands the pieces to us. Never cared much for pomegranates, but that one saved us. Then some new Arab fellows came in and sold us some good water, and pretty soon we were on our feet and on our way."

For some reason the Hermit's story of near death and survival in Arabia helped to cheer me up. If they could survive bad desert water, then surely I could survive Pat getting a telescope and me just getting a book I didn't want. Of course I could, and by the time I'd reached the dead tree on the way home, I was once again utterly deter-mined to get my archery set. I made a sacred vow to work twice as hard as before, and to stop at nothing. At the very instant I made my vow, I heard the supper bell ringing in the distance, and I took it as a sign from heaven I would succeed.

I tested my new resolve as soon as supper was over. And even though it had been a long day and I was dead tired, I managed to bring three full loads of bottles down the hill before I dragged myself off to bed.

"Tomorrow I'll bring down ten loads," I vowed.

When I came down the next morning, my parents were just finishing their breakfast.

"I let you sleep in," Mother said. "You were tired. But you'll have to get a move on. We don't want to be late."

"Late for what?" I asked.

"Church," Mother said.

"Church?" I said.

"Yes, church," she replied. "It's Sunday, isn't it? And afterward we're going to Auntie Margaret's for dinner, like always."

I felt like I'd been punched in the stomach. We hadn't gone to church since my catastrophe on the baseball field, and I'd thought we wouldn't be going again for a while. At least not until my black eye went away.

"Everyone will see my black eye!" I exclaimed.

"They won't care," she said.

"Couldn't you go and I stay here?" I pleaded.

"You're going," Father said in a firm voice.

"But I lost the game and everyone thinks I'm an idiot."

"No one thinks that at all," Mother said. "Everyone feels sorry for you."

"It was just a ball game," Father said in a softer voice. "It could have happened to anyone."

But it didn't happen to anyone. It happened to me, I thought. *And they'll never forget it.*

I went over to the mirror and saw the same old idiot looking back at me, with one black eye fading to yellow. At least Axel wouldn't be there. He didn't go to church.

Forty-five minutes later I was crammed in the truck with the rest of them, on the way to town. We still went to the little white church in Station Hill. We had no minister, however, the Reverend Hittle having abandoned us in favor of a house with indoor plumbing in Bemidji, Minnesota. There was talk that he would be replaced, but no one knew when. In the meantime, Mr. Winkfeld led the service, even though it was said by some well-informed persons that he believed people were just transferred to another planet when they died.

Mr. Winkfeld was an undertaker from Wistola, and everyone said he was a very generous man, often giving coffin discounts to needy families of people who had died. Every Sunday, without fail, he drove all the way over to Station Hill to conduct the service. He didn't preach at us, he just led the service and read the Gospel, along with a brief but uplifting article about stars or planets or what-not taken from his collection of *Sky and Telescope* magazines. This was the part of the service that Pat especially enjoyed. At certain intervals between Mr. Winkfeld's readings, Miss Scott played the small organ and led everyone in the singing of hymns.

I was in the choir, and I had enjoyed it in my former life, but now just the idea of standing up in front of everyone made me shudder. They would all have the same thought when they saw me: "There's the dummy who catches baseballs with his head."

We were among the last to arrive, and Miss Scott met us inside the door. She surprised me when she put her hand on my shoulder. She was not inclined to cozy gestures, beyond an occasional pat on the head for encouragement.

"How are you, Donald?" she asked me.

"I'm okay," I replied.

"We missed you last Sunday," she said with a smile. "The choir needs you."

Mother and Father sat down near the back, while Pat and I followed Miss Scott up the aisle. The church was packed.

Every head in every pew turned to look at me as I went forward. They seemed surprised to see me there. I guess they thought I'd be too ashamed to ever show my face in town again. The choir stared at me as I advanced toward them, and there was a small whispering buzz. Although Rachel and a few others smiled at me in an encouraging way, I knew the rest of them were remembering my humiliation.

When I turned to face the congregation, I was sure they were all thinking about what an idiot I was. A tremor ran down my back, and my knees suddenly felt weak. I was afraid I might faint.

Just in time Miss Scott started us singing a hymn, and

the congregation shuffled to its feet and joined in. This burst of activity somehow made it possible for me to survive those first awful seconds, and I knew I would make it through the ordeal. I would survive. I would survive everything they could throw at me, as long as it wasn't a baseball.

For his first reading, Mr. Winkfeld read something about forgiving those who trespass. It was a passage from the Gospel, but I felt he was talking about me. I mentally thanked him for it, and I hoped that he would go to a nice planet when he died.

There followed a long letter from Paul of Tarsus to somebody, a short article about the Triangulum Galaxy, and a story about a leper colony on an island off Australia. There was more singing, a little more praying, and then suddenly it was all over.

Usually we mingled and chatted with people after church. It was one of the few occasions when we had a chance to spend a little time with people from town. But thankfully, this time we didn't mingle or chat. We made straight for the truck, and I was greatly relieved. A minute later we were on the road, headed to Auntie Margaret's for Sunday dinner. My first public ordeal was over. I had survived. I felt relieved—and a bit dazed as well.

"How was God today?" Uncle Max asked as soon as we came through the door.

"Don't answer him," Mother said to Father—but to no avail.

"Why is it that the godless are always so interested in God?" Father wondered out loud.

"Please, you two. Don't start," Mother said.

"Are you accusing me of hypocrisy?" Uncle Max asked.

"I'm not accusing you of anything, Max. I just asked a simple question."

"You look like half a raccoon," Annie said to me, staring at my black eye.

"Annie!" Auntie Margaret exclaimed. "Is that a nice thing to say to your cousin?"

"Well, he does," Annie insisted.

"I do not!" I exclaimed.

"I'm not interested in God," Uncle Max declared.

"Well, you sure talk about Him a lot for someone who isn't interested," Father responded.

"Stop it, you two," Mother interjected.

"We're having pumpkin pie today," Auntie Margaret announced cheerfully.

"We've got a raft of pumpkins," Annie said with a smile, suddenly changing tack. "Come on, I'll show you."

Looking at pumpkins was about the last thing in the world I wanted to do, but Pat and I went outside with her. There were a lot of pumpkins out there, just as she'd said.

"We've got lots of them too," Pat said.

"I'm getting an archery set," I informed her on the way back from the pumpkins. "I'm going to become a deadly archer."

"I don't care," she responded.

This was quite disappointing. But then, Annie wasn't like other people. Things that impressed ordinary people didn't impress her much. In regard to me, nothing I ever did, or ever thought of doing, impressed her at all.

The lunch and the argument about God dragged on for what seemed like forever. Afterward they played cards in the kitchen while we did the same thing in the living room. During our game of hearts I noticed that Annie was dealing from the bottom of the deck. I then accused her of cheating, and she threw the cards in the air. The game was over.

Later in the afternoon, Annie rode her giant pig around the yard, and Uncle Max used his Kodak camera to take a picture of them. The pig's name used to be Oscar, but Annie had renamed him Pigasus after a winged horse of that name—or close to that name—that she'd read about in the book of mythology Miss Scott had given me last year. Which Annie had borrowed from me and never returned.

I was always a little afraid of Oscar—I mean Pigasus—not only because he was so big, but also because a certain look came into his eye when he saw me. I wasn't entirely sure he realized that it was people who ate pigs, and not the other way around.

On this occasion I was talked into riding him too, so I got on his back and took the reins in my hand and tried to make him go. But he wouldn't move. He just stood there like a fat statue. Uncle Max eventually took a picture of me sitting on the pig, not moving. Then Oscar—I mean Pigasus—suddenly ran forward and I fell backward off him, just as he'd planned.

As I watched Pigasus galloping away with the reins

dragging on the ground, I remembered that I'd forgotten to feed the pigs this morning. It was very important to feed them twice a day at the appointed time or they became disturbed. I usually did it right after breakfast, but all my worrying about going to church had made me forget.

When we arrived home, an eternity later, I leaped from the truck and ran upstairs to change my clothes. I had exactly one week until school started, and it was my firm intention to collect enough bottles by next Wednesday so I could buy my archery set on that day. That would give me four days to practice with it, and by that time I'd be a deadly archer—or at least I'd be well on my way.

Once I was a deadly archer, I'd make sure everyone knew about it. I had already concluded that the best way of getting the news out to the whole countryside would be to give Pat a little archery demonstration, and then tell him that he absolutely, positively, had to keep it a secret that I had become deadly with the bow and arrow. Pat never kept a secret in his life for a second longer than it took him to run to the nearest person.

"Where are you going?" Father asked me when I came down. He was at the table with a cup of coffee in his hand, reading the *True Detective* magazine Max had lent him.

"I'm going to look for some more bottles," I said.

"Did you feed the pigs this morning?" he asked very casually.

"I forgot," I said.

"Go do it right now, and don't forget again," he said in a stern voice.

On the way out to the pigpen, I began to wonder if my brain might have been permanently damaged by the blow on the head. I'd forgotten the same thing twice in the same day.

That night I went outside and nearly tripped over Pat. He was sitting on the stoop staring at the sky through his telescope. He offered to let me use it again, and it occurred to me that I was being unnecessarily stupid about it, so I took it from him and looked up at the moon, which, it seemed to me, was the only thing up there that was worth looking at.

"I'm getting up early tomorrow to look at Venus," Pat said as I handed the telescope back to him. "Want to look at it with me?"

"Is she going to be naked?" I asked.

"It's the morning star!" he cried out. "You shouldn't make jokes about stars! Stars are beautiful!"

"I hate stars," I informed him in an ice-cold voice.

CHAPTER FIVE
A Better Way

The next morning I was collecting bottles for my second trip down the hill when Charlie came over and leaned against one of the more sturdy fence posts. He took a swig of beer and squinted at me.

"How many do ya need?" he asked.

"About five hundred more," I said.

"It's gonna take ya all year." He laughed.

By now I'd come to about the same conclusion.

"You really want them bows and arrows?"

"Yeah," I said. I looked glumly down at the wagon. It seemed like a ridiculously small load.

He went back into the house, and I went back to

collecting bottles. However, a moment later he came out again with a blanket in his hand. Then he hopped aboard his old Ford truck and backed it up to the edge of the pasture where the fence was down, and he parked it there. As I looked on, he began to empty the truck box of all the junk that had accumulated in it over the years. There was a bit of everything in that truck box, including the skeleton of a dead cat.

"Her name was Calamity," he said. "I wondered where she got to."

I returned to gathering bottles while he went on cleaning out his truck. I thought he was just cleaning it out on the general principle that a truck box ought to be cleaned out every ten years or so without fail. But when it was empty, he spread the blanket over the floor and called to me.

"Load 'er up," he said. "I'm gonna help you out."

It took me a full second before I realized what he meant. He meant that I should load the truck with bottles, and he would drive them down to our place for me all at once. It would save me many days of hauling little loads down the hill. My heart leaped in my chest at the very idea of it. With Charlie's help I could still get the archery set before school started. I couldn't believe my good luck.

I worked steadily for the rest of the morning, until I couldn't lift another bottle, then I sat down on the porch and rested while Suzy cleaned my face with her tongue. I had cleared a large area, yet the truck box was still far from full. And looking around the pasture, I began to realize there weren't as many beer bottles there as I'd imagined. I just hoped there would be enough. Then Charlie came out and looked into the truck box.

"You done a lot," he commented.

"Yeah, but now I have to go home for lunch," I said.

"How many's in there?" he asked.

"I don't know. I forgot to count," I admitted.

"Don't matter. Just fill 'er up and that'll be enough. I'll move the truck over yonder to the rest of them."

I ran into my father on the way to the house.

"Guess what, Dad."

"What?"

"I don't have to haul any more bottles down the hill. Charlie's letting me load them in his truck, and he's going to drive them down for me. There'll be enough for my archery set."

"Enough for...? How many bottles has he got up there?"

"Lots and lots of them. Enough for my archery set with some left over."

"And he's giving them to you?"

"Yeah. He said I could have as many as I want."

"Schneider was right about him," Father said. "He's got a good heart."

"Yeah, does he ever!" I agreed.

"He also drinks too much beer," Father added.

After lunch was over, I went back up the hill with renewed energy. As promised, the truck had been moved to another part of the pasture, where the beer bottles were still thick on the ground. As I walked over to it Charlie came out with a sandwich and a bottle of beer. He sat down on the edge of the porch with Suzy at his side, then reached back for her bowl and poured some beer into it. She lapped it up.

I labored without letup for three hours, until I had picked up nearly all the unbroken bottles in that part of the pasture. The truck still wasn't full, so I was forced to search for bottles farther away. I staggered out for the hundredth time, pulling the wagon behind me. Once again I filled it with bottles. Once again I staggered back to the truck and unloaded the wagon. Afterward I slumped against the old truck like a deflated tire. If there were still any beer bottles left out there, they would just have to stay where they were. I was finished. I didn't have an ounce of energy left. In fact, I wasn't sure I could manage to get home. I noticed Charlie standing nearby. He downed the rest of his beer and delicately placed the empty bottle in the truck box with the rest of them.

"I'm tired," I said.

"Yeah," he agreed.

But though I was dead tired, I was all aglow inside— all aglow with warm satisfaction. I had almost done it! The truck was nearly full, and I would finish the job after supper. Along with the bottles I had piled up at home, there must be enough. Just another hour of work, and the archery set would be mine! The thought sent a little thrill up my tired spine. But after supper I was so tired that I decided to finish filling the truck in the morning.

When I reached the top of the hill the next morning, I noticed that the truck was no longer in the pasture. It was parked at the back of the house in its usual place. I ran over to it, and it was empty! All the bottles that I'd gathered were gone. The junk was back in the truck box.

I couldn't believe what I was seeing. What was going on? Did he take my bottles into Wistola without telling me? A very bad thought then entered my brain, and it made my heart stand still. Was Charlie going to keep my bottle money for himself?

CHAPTER SIX

The Archery Set

I went up to the screen door and looked in. He was in his old easy chair, with Suzy at his feet and the orange cat in his lap. He waved me inside.

"What happened to the bottles?" I asked him in a quavering voice.

"Took 'em into the city this morning," he said. "Had to go in anyways to stock up. How much you say you needed for that bow and arrow stuff?" he asked.

"Seven dollars and fifty cents," I said in a querulous voice.

He stood up and the orange cat fell to the floor. He fished in the pocket of his blue jeans with his free hand.

"Well, ya made it," he said with a grin. "They cashed in for seven dollars and sixty cents and a bit." He pulled his hand out of his pocket and counted out seven dollars and sixty-four cents into my outstretched hand.

I was overwhelmed with gratitude. I was overwhelmed with joy!

"Thanks, Charlie!" I exclaimed.

"Ain't nuthin. Maybe someday ya can help me out likewise," he said with a laugh.

I was still bubbling over with excitement when I reached home. I rushed inside to tell them the good news. "Charlie took my bottles in and I've got enough to buy it!" I exclaimed.

"That was good of him," Father said.

"What are you talking about?" Mother asked.

"Charlie Pears gave him a load of beer bottles and he took them in for him this morning," he said.

"But I picked them up and loaded them into the truck," I added. "It took a long time, but now I've got enough to buy my archery set."

"This is all news to me," she said coldly. "And I don't like it one bit."

"I'll set up some straw bales behind the chicken coop," Father informed her. "He'll only shoot the thing there. It'll be safe."

"Will you take me to town so I can buy it?" I asked her.

She didn't answer. She just stared at me.

"I'll take you in," Father said, and her stare was transferred to him.

Five minutes later we were on our way. When we reached Wistola, he drove straight to Plate's Hardware. I leaped from the truck, ran inside, and plunked my money down on the counter. Mr. Plate regarded me with raised eyebrows.

"I want to buy that archery set," I said, pointing to the wall where it was displayed in all its glory.

"I'll get it down," said Mr. Plate with a smile.

In my whole life I've never known such pure joy as I did when I put my hands on that new hardwood bow and that beautiful leather quiver with the four shiny arrows sticking out of it.

While Father looked on, Mr. Plate showed me how to string the bow. It was not an easy thing to do, but I was able to manage it on my own. A few minutes later we were back in the truck and on our way home. At that moment I was the happiest kid in the country. And Father seemed happy too.

"Don't shoot it anywhere except at the straw bales," he warned me.

"I won't," I promised him.

"And I wouldn't talk about it when your mother is around, if you know what's good for you."

"I won't."

As soon as we arrived home, I ran upstairs and borrowed Pat's red crayon. I ran to the storage shed next, where I found a suitable piece of cardboard, and I used Pat's crayon to draw some circles on it, with a solid red bull's-eye in the center. As soon as I'd finished, I ran behind the chicken coop, where Father had stacked up four straw bales. I fixed the target to the bales with a used nail, then I ran back, strung my bow, withdrew an arrow from my quiver, and I fired it off.

I missed. I missed the target. I even missed the straw bales. However, I did manage to hit the chicken coop, and when the arrow collided with the back of the building, it shattered into fragments.

It might as well have been my right arm that I was looking at, lying in pieces on the bare earth. It hurt just as much. One shot and I'd already lost one of my precious arrows. I felt like weeping. I vowed it wouldn't happen again.

And it didn't. I started again—this time much closer to the target—and I worked my way back as I improved. An hour later I'd become fairly good at it, and I was having the time of my life.

Eventually Father came by to watch me in action. "Well, I'll give you high marks for determination," he said. Then just as he was about to leave, Pat walked into the picture. Actually, he came wheeling around the corner of the henhouse like a demented chicken.

"Can I shoot it?" he asked excitedly.

He had a big grin on his face. That is, he did until I gave him the bad news.

"No, you can't. You wouldn't help me collect the bottles. Anyway, you're too young. You have to be eleven, at least." He really was too young, and knowing how careless he was, I was afraid he might break one of my precious arrows.

Even though I had given him two perfectly good reasons why he couldn't shoot my bow and arrows, he refused to accept them. He went screaming back to the house in a fit of rage. And this particular fit far exceeded the best I'd ever seen him throw. He didn't return, and I assumed Mother supported my decision.

Father had remained strangely silent during the whole episode, but after Pat had run away, he looked at me with questioning eyes.

"He wouldn't help me collect the bottles," I pointed out.

He nodded at me, a little sadly I thought, then he walked away.

I spent the rest of the afternoon practicing. Near the end of it, my drawing arm was aching, but I was happy. I knew I was well on my way to becoming a deadly archer. Pat came back and watched me for a while. I felt a slight twinge in my heart when I saw him standing there with his hair going in all directions and the little band of freckles marching across his nose. For a split second just then, I even felt that some people might possibly think I was a selfish person. However, I managed to resist the impulse to give in.

"You wouldn't help me," I reminded him, and once again he ran away with tears in his eyes.

As I walked toward the chicken coop I saw Dad going into his smokehouse. I stopped there for a moment and watched him check over the beautiful smoked ham that he'd been curing for the annual smoked ham contest in Wistola.

He turned around and looked directly at me. "You've had a good go at it," he said. "Now how about letting Pat have a try?" I hung my head and waited because I knew he was finally going to order me to share my bow and arrows with Pat. It was the end. But then in the last desperate second, I had a very cunning idea.

"It's like your ham," I said, looking up at him with tears in my eyes. "It's something really important to me, like your ham is to you."

"It's not the same thing," he said quietly. "Whatever becomes of this ham—whether it wins a prize and gets sold or we eat it ourselves—it's going to be shared by all of us." He looked calmly down at me and smiled, but he said nothing more. Instead, he put his hand on my shoulder and we walked to the house together.

The look in his eyes and the feel of his hand on my shoulder stayed with me all the way through supper. I just couldn't shake loose from it, so after supper was over and Mother and Father had gone outside to sit on the back steps with their coffee, I told Pat that he could come out with me and shoot my bow. He was ecstatic. He jumped up and down all around the kitchen, and I was barely able to keep him from kissing my hand. The commotion drew our parents back into the house.

"What's going on in here?" Mother asked.

"I told Pat he could shoot my bow and arrows," I informed her.

"He'll do nothing of the sort!"

"But he said I could!" Pat cried out.

"I don't care what he said. He's not in charge here, and you're not going to shoot that thing. Edward, say something!"

"It'll be perfectly safe," Father assured her.

"Safe? Whose side are you on?" Mother looked like she was about to have a conniption fit, but she held it in long enough to tell us to go outside.

We went outside and sat down below the window so we could listen to them argue.

"I didn't want Donald to have it in the first place, but I gave in to you on that one and look what happens. Now it's spreading over to Pat. No. I won't allow it."

"Come on, Kathleen. I'll make sure it's safe. There'll be strict rules, like we had on the rifle range in the army. I'll train them like soldiers."

"This isn't the army, and they're not soldiers. They're kids. They'll kill each other. I know it."

"I'll stay with them until—"

"Until they shoot you too," she said, finishing his sentence.

We heard Father laugh.

"You can laugh, but I'm serious."

"Look, I understand you're nervous about it. Women naturally don't take to guns or bows and arrows, but it's the kind of thing boys do. It's part of their growing up."

"Who's winning?" Pat whispered to me.

"I don't know," I said.

The argument went on and on, and Pat and I were on the verge of falling asleep when they finally came out.

"Can I shoot it now?" Pat asked.

"First, we're going to show your mother how safe it is," Father informed us. "Then, we'll see how it goes."

We headed down the lane, with Bounce jumping around us as we went forward.

"You can use my telescope anytime you want," Pat said to me along the way.

"You can shoot my bow when I'm with you," I responded in kind.

When we reached the archery range, Mother and Father and Pat stood on the sidelines, while I slowly and carefully demonstrated the science of archery by shooting my three arrows into the target. One of them hit the bull's-eye dead center, but Mother wasn't impressed.

The critical moment had now arrived. It was time for Pat to try his hand at it and prove to Mother that archery was perfectly safe.

"Now, he hasn't done it before, so you have to allow for that," Father said to her.

Mother looked at him, but she said nothing.

Father and I established a new shooting line for Pat, one very close to the straw bales. Then Father stepped back to the observer line beside Mother and I took over. I placed the bow into his hands and helped him put the arrow notch on the bowstring. I then placed his fingers correctly on the bowstring and stepped back.

"All right," I said. "Aim at the target and pull the string back slowly and then let it go."

"Okay," Pat happily agreed. He gave me a big grin, one full of love, and for a moment just then, I felt our relationship had reached a new peak of harmony. He was my friend, my brother. I would, in future, share everything I had with him.

He drew the arrow back quite well, but he experienced some difficulty in holding the bow steady long enough to take good aim at the target. In fact, when the arrow was finally released, I suspect it had no idea at all where it should go. It certainly didn't go anywhere near the target. In fact, it went up into the sky, clearing the top of the chicken coop by more than five feet.

"Missed!" Pat exclaimed, stating the obvious.

"Now I'll never find it!" I screamed.

As things turned out, however, it was not too difficult to find the arrow. When we ran around the chicken coop to the other side, we saw it immediately. It was over there in the corral, sticking out of Rodger's rear end.

Thankfully, it was only a target arrow, quite incapable of inflicting serious harm to a huge old bull like Rodger. However, Rodger didn't seem to agree. He had a very peculiar look in his eye, and he kept twitching his head back in an attempt to see what had happened down at his rear end.

"I hit Rodger," Pat said with tears in his eyes. "Is he going to die?"

"Is this all part of boys growing up?" Mother asked, turning her eyes on Father.

"Not that I remember," Father said glumly.

Rodger, who at first seemed to be taking the whole thing fairly calmly for a bad-tempered bull, now decided that something had definitely struck him in the rear end. He looked at the ground, then he snorted. Then he pawed the ground. Then he charged straight through the corral fence like it wasn't there.

"Look out!" Father cried. He tried to get us out of the path of the beast, but it wasn't necessary, because Rodger ran right past us. We would have had no chance at all if he'd been aimed at us. But fortunately, he wasn't after us. He was after the chicken coop, it seemed, having somehow got the idea it had shot him. In any case, Rodger tore through the chicken-wire fencing and attacked the unfortunate building. The air all around us was shortly filled with crazed chickens.

"Look at that!" Pat exclaimed.

"I see it!" I said.

"My chickens!" Mother cried.

We stood there staring at the rapidly disintegrating chicken coop while a cloud of feathers and chickens and dust rose up from the ground and engulfed the site. Finally, there was a creaking sound, and for the second time in living memory, the luckless chicken coop slowly collapsed.

Having successfully destroyed the chicken coop, Rodger stopped his attack. He wandered aimlessly over to the fringe of the woods with my arrow in his backside and a tangled mess of chicken-wire fencing trailing from his left horn.

While surveying the devastation, Father let loose with two powerful words he'd learned during the invasion of Europe. The first of the words was *holy*, which I think was only there to make up for the second one.

"I didn't mean to do it!" Pat cried out.

CHAPTER SEVEN

Back to Purgatory

After shaking the chicken wire from his horn, Rodger just stood at the edge of the woods, as though he were trying to remember what had happened to him. Uncle Max raised cattle and he knew all there was to know about them, so Father went off and fetched him to help with the arrow removal.

Uncle Max laughed when he saw it. When he was finished laughing, he grinned down at Pat. "You were aiming for the bull's-eye, and you got the bull's rear instead."

"I didn't mean to do it!" Pat cried for the hundredth time.

After fixing the corral and herding Rodger into it,

Uncle Max managed to pull the arrow out of Rodger without being killed. He then treated the wound, and Rodger seemed to be none the worse for wear. The most important thing of all was that Uncle Max was able to get my arrow out without breaking it. I grabbed it from him and immediately ran over to the water trough. After I'd cleaned it up, it looked as good as new.

When I awoke the next morning, my archery set was gone from the corner of the room. "I've put it away for now," Mother said when I ran downstairs to confront her. "It's too dangerous. When you're a little older, you can have it back."

I protested with all my might, but she would not be moved. Thankfully, Father was still on my side. He sent Pat and me outside, and they had a big argument over it. Unfortunately, Father and my archery set lost the argument.

"You've ruined my life!" I shrieked at Pat.

"I didn't mean to do it!" he cried.

"Just be patient for a little while," Father whispered to me later on. "You'll get it back after she's calmed down."

Rodger had always been a bad-tempered bull, but after Pat shot him, he changed. He became a nervous bull. He seemed to have become afraid of Pat, and he would wander quickly away whenever my brother appeared in the vicinity. Flight, our old plowhorse, was just the opposite. Whenever he managed to get out of the pasture, he followed Pat around just like a dog. And if Pat wasn't outside when he got loose, he would wait patiently outside the back door for him to come out.

The next day Father moved the straw bales far out into the pasture so that the arrows would just hit the ground if they missed the bales. In the meantime, Mother had calmed down, and I got my archery set back with the condition that Pat never touch it. Which was fine with me.

That same day I told Pat that I had become a deadly archer, and I warned him not to tell anyone. The next day when I checked with Rachel, she hadn't heard anything about it. Nor had anyone else over there. Pat had failed to spread my secret. All the Schneiders wanted to talk about were the details of how Rodger had got the arrow in his backside and wrecked our chicken coop. They all seemed to think it was funny.

I gave up on Pat, but that afternoon I held a special archery exhibition for Rachel and two of her sisters, in order to show them what a deadly archer looks like. I moved my firing line a little closer to the target than normal, and they all watched me put arrow after arrow in or near the bull's-eye. They seemed to like my performance, but what they really wanted to see was the wound in Rodger's backside. I gave up on them too.

The next day the school bus was at our door.

It was the same old bus as always, with the same people on it—except for Gretchen Schneider, who was now in high school, and little Tony Mansouri, who was just starting grade one. I felt a wave of dread course through me as I stepped on board.

I sat down at the very back, and the bus headed toward Station Hill, picking up more kids along the way. I listened to the excited voices from the seats in front of me, but I said nothing to anyone. I just sat there like next Sunday's chicken, thinking anxiously of what lay ahead. My black eye was gone, but the black stain on my reputation was still there.

When I stepped off the bus, Axel and his friends were waiting for me.

"Look, it's Donald Duck, the great baseball player," Axel shouted. They all burst into laughter, and their laughter spread to others. It was very hard to bear.

"Don't pay any attention to them," Rachel said to me.

Even during the opening ceremony I saw that some of the kids were sneaking peeks at me. It was a relief when we took our places in the classroom.

There were a few changes this year. Gretchen and the rest of last year's grade eights were gone. Except for Andy Sims and Arlene Millan, everyone had advanced by one grade, and there were six new grade ones in attendance, including Tony. But otherwise, everything was exactly the same.

Miss Scott read the rules of the school and explained them in detail. We sang some songs together, and the morning of the first day of school went forward, step by step, in exactly the same fashion as it had last year. I felt like I'd gone back in time. I knew I hadn't, of course. A lot of things had happened since last year. For one thing, I'd grown six inches taller. For another, I had lost my reputa-tion and my honor.

Every year Miss Scott put on a Gilbert and Sullivan

operetta with her students, and she was soon introducing us to our new one. The operetta was originally written for adults, so she'd spent the summer shrinking it down and making it right for kids to perform.

"This year we'll be doing *The Pirates of Penzance*," she informed us. "It's full of fun. You'll love it. We'll be doing it in the spring, so we're going to have to work very hard to make sure we're ready by then. You already know some of the songs, so we've got a head start. Now for some great news. We'll be doing the performance in the church, which will give us more room to work in. Okay, let's listen to some of the songs."

While Miss Scott was winding up her Victrola, Axel looked back and smirked at me. I liked to sing, and for some reason he'd always made fun of me for it. I stared straight ahead, as though I didn't see him.

I hated Axel, but there were lots of kids in the school who admired him—especially the girls. He was very sure of himself, and he had good teeth. He smiled a lot because he liked to show them off. But what really grated on me was that in addition to being confident and good-looking, he was very good at math. When I managed to scrape by with 50 percent in a math test, he would be flying high above me with a lofty 60 or 70. It was my bad luck that we were in the same grade.

There was only one thing concerning Axel Smart that pleased me. It was a feeling I had that, deep down inside the hidden part of her heart, Miss Scott didn't like him either.

I had been dreading the lunch hour, but when it came,

nothing much happened. We just filed outside to eat, and contrary to my expectations, Axel and his friends ignored me. While they headed to the old picnic tables over by the caragana bushes to eat their lunches, I went in the opposite direction and sat down next to Andy Sims, alongside the pipe-rail fence at the front of the school.

About the only thing Andy and I had in common was that we went to the same school. Andy was not a talkative person, and that was fine with me. I didn't want to talk to anyone.

A few minutes later, after their sandwiches had been devoured and their jars of milk were empty, Axel and the other boys at the picnic tables headed for the baseball field. Others were already out there throwing the ball around, and I felt a terrible pang in my heart. I wanted to be out there with them, but it could never be. I had taken a blood oath that I would never play baseball again, and I never went back on my word.

Henry Adamson came around the corner of the school and walked over to me.

"Come on, let's go," he said.

"I'm not playing baseball anymore," I informed him.

He smiled and shook his head.

"You've got to be kidding. Come on," he urged me. "You can take Conrad's place."

Conrad had played shortstop on the Blue team last year, but he had moved on to high school and the slot was vacant.

Henry didn't give up easily. He told me that missing

that catch didn't matter. "It was just a game," he said, and he tried hard to talk me into playing, but I steadfastly refused.

"I thought there was more to you," he said finally. He shook his head, then turned around and headed for the field. As I watched him go, I was overwhelmed with a feeling of failure. I would have wept if I'd been a weepy kind of kid.

"Ain't you playin' ball no more?" Andy asked.

His voice startled me.

"No, I'm finished with it," I said.

"Is it 'cause you got hit on the head?" he asked.

"Yeah," I said. When dealing with Andy, the simpler the explanation, the better.

When I came out of the school at the end of the day, I heard a voice from nearby.

"Hey, Donald Duck, how come you weren't out there today?"

It was Axel, of course, accompanied by his grinning ninny friends.

"I'm not playing anymore," I said.

"Oh no!" he exclaimed. "Then how're you going to make it into the big leagues like your uncle Danny?"

I wanted to punch him in the mouth, but I knew what that would mean. In the first place, he'd probably take me to pieces, and in the second place, Miss Scott did not tolerate fighting, and she enforced the rule rigidly with her bum paddle. The punishment had been administered once during the previous year to a pair of grade-seven boys. I didn't see it, but I'd listened from outside, below the windows, with the rest of the school. It wasn't a pretty sound, and the paddling was followed by a week's expulsion from school. For that reason fights only occurred during the summer vacation, or when the school was closed for Christmas or other such celebrations of peace and brotherhood.

I turned away and walked around to the front of the school, where I joined up with the kids waiting for our bus. But Axel and his cronies followed me. I heard their voices again, shouting above the chatter of the crowd.

"His mommy don't want him to play baseball anymore," one of them yelled.

"'Cause he might get clunked on the head again," another added.

The last comment was followed by a burst of laughter.

"Maybe he can play volleyball with the girls," Vincent Slade said. Vincent lived only a mile or so to the north of us and we might have been friends, if we hadn't hated each other. His comment was followed by another burst of laughter from Axel and his crowd. Then my cousin Annie suddenly turned toward them and shouted, "Up yours!"

This stunned them for a moment. However, they quickly rallied with a frenzied burst of catcalls and shouts. Fortunately, the bus arrived just then.

"What does 'up yours' mean?" Rachel asked Annie after we got underway.

"Figure it out," Annie said brusquely.

I knew what it meant, but I didn't bother to tell Rachel.

I didn't feel like talking to anyone. I just sat there in a gloomy haze all the way home.

Everyone in the school had heard about Rodger getting shot in the rear end. In fact, everyone in the county had heard about it, but no one seemed to have heard about the fact that I'd become a deadly archer. It didn't seem to matter at all. After all my hard work, I got nothing in return. Except that shooting arrows was fun.

The taunting from Axel and his cronies went on and on, and by the time the week was over, I hated school so much that I actually considered jumping off the barn in order to break a leg and escape from it. However, there was always the possibility that I might accidentally kill myself in the process, and I was afraid to die. I was afraid I'd go straight to hell, having committed a whopping great sin by relentlessly hating Axel day and night with all my heart. I knew full well you're supposed to turn the other cheek to your enemies, even though it's an unnatural thing to do.

In the end I didn't have to do anything drastic to my body because, much to my surprise, the mockery and the teasing from Axel and his crowd simmered down after a few weeks. They got tired of it and more or less ignored me. So did everyone else.

I had become a nobody. That was an improvement, but I was still not happy with my life. I still felt a wave of humiliation sweep over me whenever I remembered my terrible failure in August. However, little did I know that something spectacular was about to happen that could change everything.

CHAPTER EIGHT
Salvation

The harvest was near. Our fields were a golden sea in the autumn sun, and everything was fine on the home front. But then, unexpectedly, a serious argument broke out in the kitchen. I had just come back from the outhouse. Mother was peeling potatoes and Father was sitting at the table when I came in. I went over to the washbasin, and I had just begun to wash my hands when he said, "I'm afraid I'm going to need your help again this year."

"What?"

"I'll need you to drive the truck when the harvesting starts."

"No," she said. "You promised it was only for the first year and you'd never ask me again."

"Yes, but—"

"You never go back on your word," she interrupted. "Remember?"

"I'm not going back on my word. All I said was I need your help. I didn't actually ask you for it."

She paused in her peeling, and there was a puzzled expression on her face.

"Well then, that's the end of the discussion," she said.

He smiled at her.

"But if you were to do it willingly, without me actually having to ask you, then I wouldn't be going back on my word, would I?"

"Don't be ridiculous. If I were willing, we wouldn't be arguing about it."

"We're not arguing about it. I'm just telling you that we don't have the money to hire anyone, and if I have to do it by myself, we stand a chance of losing half the crop because I might not get it all in before the frost."

He looked glumly out the window.

"Eddie, I did it once for you," she said more softly. "But I can't do it again. I just can't."

I stared at her. For the life of me, I couldn't figure out why she wouldn't do it. She drove the truck all the time. She drove it into Wistola every Saturday for the market. I couldn't understand her at all.

"The electricity is coming next summer," he said. "But

we won't be able to afford it if I don't get all the crop in before it freezes."

There was no answer. The argument was over as far as she was concerned.

"Ah well," he sighed. "If I don't make it, at least we won't have to waste any money on indoor plumbing. Without electricity, you can't have indoor plumbing."

When Father headed outside, I trailed along behind him. I was very puzzled by what I'd heard.

"Why won't she drive the truck?" I asked him as we went into the machine shed.

"Okay, I'll tell you," he said gravely, "but don't talk about it to your mother. In fact, don't talk about it to anyone, especially not Pat. Understand?"

"I won't," I promised.

"You know your mother grew up on a farm with Aunt Margaret and Aunt Helen and your uncle Danny. You know their mom died when they were little, so their father—your grandfather—raised them by himself."

"I know," I said.

"He was a very fine man. They all loved him, but your mother most of all. And he doted on her. Anyway, they all worked together, and they made a go of it on their farm."

I knew quite a bit about her life on the farm. She'd told me stories about it when I was young. "She had a horse named Babe," I said.

"Yes. And she had a little Scottie dog too. Anyway, it happened one day when they were in the middle of the harvest."

"What happened?" I asked.

"If you'll hold your horses, you'll find out," he said. "She was driving the truck for her father while he was combining," he continued. "She was just sixteen at the time. Anyway, they'd worked through the morning, and they'd just stopped for lunch when his sandwich fell out of his hand and he keeled over. She tried to revive him, but he wouldn't come out of it, so she jumped in the truck and roared over to the house. Then your aunt Helen took off in the truck to get the doctor, and Auntie Margaret and your mother ran back to the field. But none of it did any good. His old ticker had just given it up. He was dead."

"Oh," I murmured.

"To make things even worse, when your mom had driven in from the field to get help, she'd run over her little Scottie dog. He'd been sleeping under the truck, and she'd forgotten about him."

"Was he dead?" I asked.

"He was a pancake," Father said grimly.

"Oh," I said.

"So that's why she hates driving the truck out in the field at harvesttime," he said. "It brings back those bad memories."

At that very instant, despite the tragic story, my own personal sun broke through the ceiling in the machine shed and illuminated the whole place with a brilliant light.

"I could drive the truck!" I exclaimed.

He looked at me and smiled. I could see in his eyes

that he didn't take my suggestion seriously. "Maybe next year, when you're a little bigger," he said.

"But I can reach the pedals! I can do it!" I insisted.

He looked at me, this time more thoughtfully.

"I can do it," I insisted. He looked me over again, as though he were sizing me up, then he smiled. "I guess it wouldn't hurt if I gave you a few lessons, just to see how you make out."

"Really?"

"Well, we'll give it a try and see how it goes."

"When?"

"After I get this thingamajig bent back the way it's supposed to be."

I was suddenly full of hope. This was big! Three of the grade-eight farm boys were excused from school during the harvest in order to drive trucks for their fathers, and it made them seem like men. And soon I would be among them. One of the chosen few. And I was only in grade six! No one would ever look at me in the same way again. And best of all, this was something Axel and the other town kids would never be able to do.

"Just one thing. Don't mention this to your mother," he cautioned.

"Why not?"

"Never mind. Just don't, that's all."

"Okay," I said.

"Now don't go getting your hopes up," he warned me. "This is just going to be a little practice, and that's all."

I found Pat up in the loft, sleeping on the hay.

"Wake up!"

He opened his eyes and looked up at me.

"Guess what?" I said. I had been holding my fantastic news in my belly all the way up to the loft, and it had swelled up to the point of explosion.

"What?"

"I'm going to drive the truck for Dad!" I exclaimed. "I'm going to haul the wheat in from the field like Mom did last year."

"Can I help?" he asked.

"No, you're way too young," I informed him with a contemptuous glance. "You have to be eleven."

I could see the disappointment spread over his face, and I felt sorry for him. But it wasn't my fault he was only seven.

On the way down from the loft, it occurred to me that even though I'd fooled around with the gearshift when the truck wasn't running, and even though I'd driven the truck in low gear out in the pasture a few times with my father sitting at my side, I had no practical experience driving it all by myself. For just a second I wondered if I'd bitten off more than I could chew. "No! I can do it!" I told myself.

I wandered around the yard until I saw my father come out of the machine shed.

"Go get in the truck," he said.

I let out a whoop of joy and ran to the truck ahead of him. I was about to jump in the passenger side when he shouted at me.

"Get in the driver's seat."

I climbed aboard and sat there, my heart thumping like a berserk pile driver. I was happy and excited beyond... I actually couldn't think of anything in my life beyond it. My days of humiliation would soon be over. My honor would soon be restored.

When he opened the other door and climbed in beside me, Pat appeared from nowhere and climbed in next to him.

"Is he going to drive it for the harvest?" he asked.

I was once again reminded that I should never say anything at all about anything at all to my brother unless I wanted it to be broadcast throughout the nation.

"No, he's not," Father said, frowning at me. "We're just practicing."

I put my hands on the steering wheel. My heart was going at seventy-five miles an hour, and there was not a single thought in my head about Axel, school, baseball, or anything else.

"You know how to start it," he said. "Make sure it's in neutral, then pull out the choke and push the start button."

I was about to comply when I saw Mother approaching us with giant strides, and there was a look on her face that would have frightened a Hun off his horse. When she went around to Father's side, he looked down at her through the open window.

"I know what you're doing and it won't work!" she exclaimed.

"I'm just teaching him how to drive it and nothing else," he said gruffly.

"You know he's too young," she said fiercely. "He'll have an accident."

She spoke with such conviction that I began to worry. I knew that every year, without fail, farm accidents killed a lot of children. Would I be the next to die?

"I'm only teaching him to drive it around the field. He has to learn sometime, so why not now?" he said grimly.

"Because he's only eleven years old, that's why not!" Mother exclaimed.

"He's tall enough to reach the pedals," Father responded.

"I'll be twelve next March," I reminded her.

She ignored my comment. Instead, she fixed her eyes on him, and they were like burning spears.

"Don't try that one on me," she warned him.

I didn't understand what she meant and I expected the argument to continue, but she just stared hard at him for a second, then turned away and marched back to the house.

This seemed to make him very angry. His face had turned all red.

"One important thing," he said in a low voice. "When you're working with machinery, even if it's just driving the truck, it's important to remain calm at all times."

"I will," I promised.

"Okay. Now pull out the choke and push the button," he said.

I pulled the choke out and pushed the button. The starter whirled and the motor turned over and the old truck coughed once, then twice more, then it caught on and shuddered back to life. It was an old bull, that truck. I could feel its massive strength as it shook itself awake beneath me.

"Let it warm up a bit, then you can push the choke in," he said.

A moment later I pushed the choke in. The truck was now idling in its usual fashion, rumbling and vibrating like a volcano on the verge of erupting. It also gave me the peculiar notion that it was leaning a little to one side, as if that were the direction it was going to explode in someday when it finally decided to kill us all.

"Okay, that's good," he said. "Now, what do you do next?"

I knew what to do next, but somehow being asked to say it in words confused me and made me forget.

"Just relax," he said. "I'll show you everything and we'll just do one thing at a time. It's not hard. It's just a matter of practicing. Practice makes perfect," he said. "Now, push the clutch in."

Then I remembered it all. I stretched out and pushed the clutch in, then I tried to shift into low gear, as I'd seen my father and mother do a hundred times. No, a thousand times.

"Right. Right. That's it."

But it wasn't quite "it." I knew what to do, but I couldn't make the gears slip into low. He put his hand over mine and guided me into it.

"Keep the clutch in. Hands on the steering wheel. Get ready. I want you to drive toward the gate. Ready?"

"Yes," I said nervously. It was hard to keep the clutch in and look out the window at the same time. Once the clutch was out, I could lift my body up a bit and it would be better.

"Now, slowly let the clutch out and give it a bit of gas as you do it. Clutch and gas. Clutch and gas. But slowly. Slowly."

When I released the last bit of the clutch, I did it too quickly. The truck lurched forward and the motor abruptly died.

"You have to let it out more slowly," he said with a patient smile. "Let's try it again."

I spent the rest of that wonderful day learning how to drive the truck around the field. I did manage to knock over a fence post, but the tires missed the barbs in the wire and there was no damage, except to the post.

There was just one thing that made driving it a little difficult. It was that I had to stretch myself out like a rubber band whenever I had to use the clutch, because I had to push it right down to the floor. Using the brake was easier because I didn't have to push it in all the way. I only had to touch the gas pedal with my toe to keep the truck going, since we went everywhere at low speeds.

Supper wasn't ready when we went in for it. In fact, Mother wasn't even in the kitchen, so Father made us some sandwiches, which we ate out in the yard, sitting in the early evening sunlight on the back of the truck with the tailgate down. It was very enjoyable. The humiliation of the last few months now seemed far away, and I felt good inside myself, like I was a solid person again.

The next morning Mother was back to cooking for us, but the temperature in the kitchen was well below freezing.

On Monday at recess, Slade and Axel and a few others were lounging around the entrance when I came out.

"I heard you're going to drive the truck for your pa," Slade said.

Pat! Once again he had telegraphed the news in every direction. I vowed never to tell him anything for the rest of his life—and beyond, if possible.

"The Duck has to do something," Axel commented with a snide smile. "Since he can't play baseball."

I didn't care one whit about Axel's scorn. I didn't care, because I knew he envied me. And so did everyone else. As the day went on, I saw something new in everyone's eyes. Surprise? Yes, absolutely. No one my age was driving a truck. Admiration? Certainly. From most of them, at least. Naturally my chest was sticking out a mile in front of me. I was back. I was me again. Only bigger and better.

I wondered if Miss Scott had heard the news. If not, she soon would because my father would be asking her to let me miss school during the harvest. She wouldn't like it. She didn't like it with the others, but it was the one time when farm needs were more important than school.

As soon as I got home, I leaped off the bus and went looking for Father. He came out from behind the combine and we went straight at it. A few minutes later I was bringing the truck into position to back up to the auger. This was a serious business and required my full concentration.

Our grain auger was basically a long metal pipe with an attached motor and a gigantic corkscrew thing that turned inside the pipe. Through its lower mouth, it took the wheat from the pile where it was unloaded from the truck, and it lifted it up into the granary through a little door near the top and deposited it there through its upper mouth. It would do the same thing with a hand or foot, if one got careless around it.

I started out fairly well, using the clutch and gas together to slowly back up to the auger. There was a pole set up to help guide me into it, but of all the things I'd learned to do in the last three days, this was definitely the most difficult. I had to stretch myself as far as I could in order to handle the clutch and look through the side mirror at the same time.

As I was backing up, slowly and steadily, I was imagining how Axel must have felt when he'd first heard that I was driving the truck for my father. But then, just as I was enjoying a small thrill of happiness at the thought, my foot slipped off the clutch. I reacted immediately by trying to hit the brake with my right foot, but I missed it on the first try. A second later, I slammed on the brake and the motor immediately died and the truck stopped, but it was too late. When I ran back, I saw that the edge of the truck box had gone into the auger's motor. It had hit the carburetor, which was the most important and vulnerable part of the whole machine. Father was already peering into it, examining the damage.

"You smashed it," Pat said.

Tears welled up in my eyes. I had a sudden vision of the crop freezing and the bank taking our farm away. All because of my carelessness.

"My foot slipped off the clutch," I said.

Father put his hand on my shoulder and patted it gently.

"Accidents happen," he said. "I've had my share of them."

After he'd moved the truck away from the auger, he examined the damaged carburetor more closely while I stood beside him and stared fixedly at it. I waited with stomach-turning anxiety for his verdict.

"Orville can fix it," he said finally.

I started to breathe again.

He quickly detached the mashed carburetor, and a few minutes later, we were on our way down the road.

Orville Bjorken—BJ for short—lived a few miles west of us. Mr. Schneider said that he could fix anything mechanical, and fortunately, Mr. Schneider was right. For just two dollars, BJ fixed the carburetor as good as new. I was heartsick over what had happened, but at least I had not put the crop in danger.

The next day when I got home from school, I went in search of my father. I was hoping against hope that he would give me another chance, but the look in his eyes told me everything.

"Aren't I going to drive anymore?" I asked him.

"Sorry, kiddo," he said. "Next year, maybe. You'll be taller then, so it'll be a lot easier."

Everything was suddenly ruined. I would not be driving back from the fields with the truck loaded with grain and my heart loaded with triumph. I would not be taking two weeks off school to do the vital work, like the older boys. I'd let myself down, and another horrible humiliation was coming my way. I was back to being the school's number one dunce.

"But everybody knows. At school…"

He put his hand on my shoulder and smiled down at me.

"You shouldn't have told them."

"It was Pat."

"Well, you shouldn't have told him, either. You shouldn't have jumped to conclusions."

My world had changed so abruptly that I felt dizzy. For a second just then, I thought I was going to faint. Tears flooded my eyes.

He drew me over to him and hugged me. It was a rare moment, for he was not a hugging type of person.

"You did your best. That's what really matters," he said. "And you did very well for your age."

It didn't help. Nothing could help me now.

I had a troubled sleep that night—the night I ceased to be a truck driver. I had disturbed dreams. Sometimes I thought I heard whispers, but they were just phantom whispers, leftovers from the dreams. But once I woke up and heard real whispers. They were coming from the register. I got out of bed and crept over to it to listen. I knew immediately that they were talking about me.

"Life's full of disappointments," he said. "He'll just have to learn to live with them, like the rest of us."

"I know, but ... There's been ... You know. So much ..."

"He'll survive," he said.

"This is your fault," she said.

"Yes, it is and I'm sorry. I'll drive the truck myself from now on, until Donald's old enough to do it—risk of frost or not. Do you forgive me?"

"Of course I forgive you," she said.

After a moment's silence, she spoke again.

"There's just one more thing," she said.

"What's that?"

"I'll drive the truck this year."

"No you won't," he quickly answered.

"Yes, I've been thinking about it. I shouldn't let those old memories—"

"I said no, and I mean it," he interrupted. "You're not driving it!"

"Don't raise your voice," she whispered harshly. "You'll wake the kids."

"All right, but you're not doing it," he said in a firm voice.

"Eddie, seriously ... I'm over it. He died out there in the field, but he could just as easily have died washing the dishes. Not that he ever washed a dish in his life. I mean this is all so ... I've been so ... I mean refusing to drive the truck when you need me. It's stupid and it's selfish, and I'm not going to let those old memories get the best of me anymore. So I'm driving. I'm driving the truck this year, and whenever you need me. Now, don't argue with me."

"Okay," he said. "If that's the way you really feel." There was a moment of silence before he spoke again. "Darling," he said, "I love you."

Axel was overjoyed when he heard the news about me. "Can't play baseball. Can't drive a truck. Gosh, what'll Uncle Danny think about this?" he said at recess when I came outside. There was a tremendous wave of laughter.

"Maybe he can play volleyball with the girls," someone else yelled. It was Vincent Slade.

"That's an old one, Slade," I said in a cold voice, staring right at him. He emitted a weak laugh and looked away.

"Oh boy, he's a tough one," Axel said, pretending to cower away from me. And everyone laughed again.

The only bright spot in my life was that Miss Scott picked me to play the part of the Pirate King in our operetta, *The Pirates of Penzance*. It was a major part, although it wasn't the leading part. The leading male part—the role of Frederick—went to Vincent Slade. I didn't care. I preferred to be the Pirate King. If I had been one in real life, I would have made Axel and all his cronies walk the plank.

Annie was hoping to get the leading female part— Mabel. It wasn't because she wanted to sing a duet with

Vincent Slade. She also hated him. She just wanted the lead role because she liked being the center of attention. But the part of Mabel went to Marjorie Laroque, who sang better than Annie and was about seven and a half times as nice. Hannah Donnelly got the part of Ruth, Frederick's old nurse. This was also a major part, and she was overjoyed about it. As for Annie, she got to be one of the Major-General's daughters. This was only a minor role, and she was not happy.

My brother was selected to be one of the policemen in the operetta, which in real life would have been the occupation he was least suited for. Axel was also one among the crowd of policemen. As far as singing went, he was at his best when his mouth was shut.

A few days later when I was about to go outside for lunch, Miss Scott called me back and gave me a book.

"You don't have to bring it back," she said.

I looked at her, not understanding.

"It's a gift," she said. "I hope you enjoy it."

It was called *The Arabian Nights*. It contained stories that a lady named Scheherazade told her husband when she tucked him into bed at night. One a night was what he got. And as a reward for telling him an interesting story every night, she got to keep her head for another day.

There were stories about Aladdin and his magic lamp, Ali Baba and the Forty Thieves, Sinbad the Sailor, and many others. I'd already read them somewhere else—most of them, at least—but I didn't tell Miss Scott.

As usual, I ate my lunch with Andy by the pipe-rail fence

out front. Afterward I opened the book and discovered that Miss Scott had written something in the front of it:

Dear Donald, Always remember that out of every failure a greater success may come, although it may come from a different direction.

Miss Scott

I knew that she was just trying to make me feel better about what had happened to me. I appreciated it, but it didn't help.

On the way home I remembered that I still had a pile of bottles left behind the lilacs, and that night I asked Father if he'd take them in for me. He said he would, but he didn't have time to do it right away, because the harvest was about to start.

It started on Saturday. There had been no rain at all; however, in the early morning the wheat was damp from the overnight dew, so it was necessary to wait for the sun to dry it. Otherwise the damp wheat would plug up the combine, which would hold things up even longer.

As soon as the wheat was dry enough, he drove the combine out to the fields, and the truck tagged along behind it with Mother at the wheel. Father went about his business quietly and purposefully, but there was a powerful excitement in his eyes, and something of his excitement seemed to spill over and infect Pat and me. For the first time since my accident with the carburetor, I felt a little bit happy.

I *was* given a job to do; but it was work of little importance. All I did was start up the auger when Mother came in with a load, then use one of the scoop shovels to help her push the grain off the truck and shovel it into the auger's mouth.

Pat had nothing at all to do except stay clear of the auger and ride around in the truck to keep Mother company. In between times, while I waited for the truck to come back, I read a book called *The Tower Treasure*. It was about two brothers called the Hardy Boys, and it was a great book. I read it twice that day, and I could hardly wait to get back to the Carnegie Library in Wistola and get some more like it. There was a whole row of them in there, I remembered happily. Reading books was the one good thing I had left.

At about two in the afternoon, I was sent to bring the lunch basket from the cooling shelf in the basement, and the combining stopped briefly for lunch. I don't know why, but sandwiches taste better when they're eaten out in the field during the harvest.

One night Father paid a visit to Mr. Schneider, and he was smiling when he came home. "Schneider says the price is good," he said. "And it looks to be steady."

I asked him what he meant.

"He means our life is going to get a lot better," Mother answered for him.

"But let's not count our horses before they're hatched," he said with a grin.

"It's chickens," Mother said.

"What chickens?" Pat asked.

"Your father's chickens," she said. "He's changed them into horses."

"What horses?" he asked.

"The ones that used to be chickens," she said.

One afternoon Miss Scott took us over to the church to sing through the whole operetta. On the way back to the school when the practice was over, I had a powerful inspiration. I had the role of Pirate King, and I decided I would sing it so magnificently that I'd make everyone forget about my humiliation on the ball field and my failure as a truck driver. The excitement welled up in me at the thought of it. It was the answer I'd been searching for. People might not have noticed that I had become a deadly archer, but there was no way they could overlook an amazing pirate king who was singing his heart out right in front of them.

When I got home from school, I sang the "Pirate King Song" while I fed the pigs. Again and again I sang it as I wandered around the place, until the supper bell summoned me away from my ship.

CHAPTER NINE
Wealth

One day Mother was sitting on the step when we got home from school. Cannibal, our cat, was in her lap and there was a cup of coffee in her hand. There was also a big grin on her face.

"It's all finished," she said happily. "Your father just took the first load in, and the rest of it is in the bins."

A second later our truck came roaring into the yard, and Father leaped down from it like Errol Flynn in Robin Hood. He came toward us, smiling broadly. Then without warning, he took Mother in his arms and whirled her around. "It's nearly three bucks a bushel on the Chicago exchange!" he exclaimed. "Do you know what that means?"

"What?"

"It means we're rich!"

"You're kidding."

"I'm not. It's true. It's three bucks a bushel," he assured her.

"What's three bucks a bushel?" Pat asked. As usual, he was a full page behind the rest of us.

"The price of wheat," Father said with a grin.

"Lord on high!" Mother exclaimed.

"I'm going to haul the rest of it in right away," he said. "If I can get anything like that for all of it, we'll be able to catch up with the mortgage and still have enough for the electricity when it comes next summer. We'll even have enough to buy an electric pump and a pressure tank and a line to the kitchen, and then you'll have a real kitchen sink. Who knows, we might even have enough for an indoor bathroom!"

"Oh Lord, let it be so!" Mother exclaimed.

They whirled again in each other's arms, and Pat began to dance around them. Meanwhile, Bounce was jumping all over the place like a demented dog—which he was, actually. As for me, I remained quite calm. On the outside, at least. But inside I was trying to think of what I wanted most in the world.

Arrows, I thought. *I'll get them to buy me some more arrows, then later on I can use my bottles for something else.*

"One thing I'm going to get for sure," Father said.

"What?" Mother asked.

"Apple trees," he said. "Two of them."

"I'm getting my electric washing machine," she informed him. "I've already saved half of what I need for it, so that's extra money."

"What will happen to Siegfried?" Pat asked worriedly.

Siegfried was Mother's gas-powered washing machine. It did the job; however, when fully loaded it had a tendency to walk around on its own, like a mechanical Frankenstein.

"We'll point him toward Germany and let him go," she said. "He'll enjoy the walk."

"Of course, you can't grow good eating apples here," Father said thoughtfully. "But they'll be good enough for cooking and juicing. An apple tree is like money in the bank."

"Just to take a bath in a real bathtub," Mother said dreamily.

Now, finally, it was my turn.

"Can I get some more arrows?" I asked.

"We'll see," he said.

"I want a rabbit," Pat interjected.

"Then go catch one," Father responded.

All of us laughed at that, including Pat.

But then Father turned serious. "Before we do anything else, we have to pay the arrears on the mortgage," he reminded us. "So there goes a big chunk of it right off the bat."

"And we need to put enough aside to live on until the next crop comes in," Mother pointed out.

And with that, we started to go back down the hill we'd just climbed.

"Yeah," Father agreed. "We can't go off spending money in all directions. We can handle the necessities, but we have to save the rest for when the electricity comes next year."

"When we get electricity, we'll be able to listen to the radio again. Don't forget that," Mother said.

"We haven't *got* a radio," Pat pointed out.

"We'll get one," Father said.

"And that's a promise," Mother added happily.

Listening to *The Shadow* and *Fibber McGee and Molly* and *The Charlie McCarthy Show*, and all the other programs I loved so much when we lived in Wistola, would be a big improvement in my life. And having an indoor bathroom would be wonderful too, especially in the winter.

"I'll have to get busy after supper and get Maggie loaded for the morning," Father said to Mother. "I want to get an early start."

"Yes," she agreed. "There's sure to be long lineups at the elevator when everyone hears about the price."

Early the next morning, even before the school bus had arrived, Father had already begun to haul our grain to the Station Hill elevator. This went on for several days without letup, and when it was all delivered, he was very happy with the price he'd gotten for it.

We celebrated our good fortune by going into Wistola one night and seeing a movie called *Cloak and Dagger*, starring Gary Cooper. Father admired Gary Cooper because he didn't talk much unless he had to, and he never bragged about himself. You knew what he was by what he did. It was a great movie, full of spies and Nazis.

I got my arrows, as promised—four of them! I did have to wait a week for them to come into Plate's Hardware, but once I got my hands on them, they made target practice much more enjoyable. Pat got a kitten instead of a pet rabbit, but he was satisfied with that. He named it Helen after our aunt Helen, who lived in Chicago. I thought it was stupid to call her that. I didn't want to be reminded of my aunt Helen every time I saw his cat. It wasn't that I didn't like my aunt Helen. She'd once given me a pair of rubber boots, and I did like her. But not that much.

Things at school had settled down again, and I'd become resigned to that gray, unsmiling part of my world. It didn't bother me very much anymore—except for the lunch hour. I hated seeing and hearing the guys out there playing baseball. I hated it so much that I took to wandering over to the scrawny town park to eat my lunch and read.

When it was raining, I had to stay indoors and eat with everyone else, and I truly hated that. I hated their noise. I hated their laughter. I hated how happy and comfortable everyone seemed to be, except for me. I just sat at my desk, ate my lunch, read my book, and tried to ignore them all.

Every day as soon as I got home, I sang the "Pirate King Song" to the pigs, and I could feel myself getting better and better at it. When I wasn't singing or doing chores, I was usually practicing with my bow and arrows or reading. I'd read all the Hardy Boys books in the Wistola library, and I was now reading them for the second time. How I wished I could have lived in their world. It was so much better than mine.

At school I did eventually work my way through to a reasonable understanding of the whys and wherefores of fractions, but more than once along the way, the whole sad business, coupled with Axel's smirking looks in my direction, made me feel like the school dunce.

One day Axel and his friends were passing by the volleyball court on their way to the entrance. Annie and Hannah were tightening the net as they went by. I was following along with some other kids, a few paces behind Axel and his crew.

Hannah was a big girl in the seventh grade, and she possessed an even bigger heart. I'd never known anyone like her. Her smile was pure sunshine, and waves of goodwill radiated out from her. She lived on a farm near Uncle Max's, so she and Annie had known each other all their lives. They weren't close friends, however. Although Annie liked her in small doses, she could only take so much of Hannah's sunshiny personality before it began to grate on her. But everything annoyed Annie, sooner or later. As for Hannah, she loved Annie—a difficult thing to accomplish for most people, but Hannah somehow managed it.

A long time ago Axel Smart had invented his own name for Hannah. He called her the Sunshine Mountain because she was so big and so cheerful. And whenever he said "Look, there goes the Sunshine Mountain," Axel and his cronies would laugh at her.

Axel had never called Hannah that belittling name where she could hear him say it. He just said it to his friends—and to whoever happened to be in the vicinity. But that day as he was passing by the volleyball court with Emmanuel and Martin, he smiled at her and said, "How's the Sunshine Mountain today?" There was the usual laughter from his pals.

It took Hannah a full second to understand what he'd said—or rather what he'd meant, but as soon as she understood it, her face went pale and her eyes gleamed with moisture. She dropped the cord she was holding and ran behind the school.

"You creep!" Annie hissed at him.

The venomous look in Annie's eyes startled everyone there, including me. But Axel quickly recovered.

"She's going to beat me up. I'm *so* afraid," he said with a laugh. His pals quickly joined in the laughter.

I liked Hannah. I felt bad for her, and I might have said something to Axel myself, but Annie had already said it.

"What are you looking at?" Axel said to me with sudden fierceness.

"I'm not looking at anything," I said.

"You're going to get yours," he snarled.

He raised his fist and waved it in front of me.

"Buzz off," Annie said. Her hands were on her hips, her eyes were ablaze, and she looked like she was ready to go to war.

Axel looked at her, and for just a split second he

seemed a little befuddled. He recovered quickly and managed to emit a hollow laugh. The remarkable thing was that he moved on without saying anything back to her.

When Hannah came into the classroom, she was smiling as though nothing had happened, but I knew too well what she was really feeling.

Axel was a genuine puzzle to me. He had everything going for him, and he could be very agreeable when he wanted to be. So why did he enjoy making fun of people? Everyone would have liked and admired him if only that rotten part of his brain could have been surgically removed.

Suddenly, the Harvest Dance was upon us. Almost everyone came to it, and they all said it was the best dance ever. In fact, they were already saying it when the dance had barely started. However, it wasn't really because the dance was so great. It was because the price of wheat had put everyone in a jolly mood—everyone except me.

I danced with Miss Scott early on, and I put forward my opinion that the world would be a better place if fractions could be entirely avoided by rounding things off instead of having bits and pieces of pie and other stuff left over at the end. She laughed at my suggestion, but she wasn't able to offer me a good reason for keeping things as they were. Afterward, I danced with Rachel, but I accidentally stepped on her foot. This time I actually hurt it.

"Sorry," I said as she knelt down to rub it.

"I noticed you didn't step on Miss Scott's foot," she remarked bitterly.

"Her feet are smaller than yours," I said.

It was a joke, of course. I thought it was a pretty good one too because it was different from the kind of jokes I usually made. Rachel didn't care for it, however. She abandoned me in the middle of the dance floor. I wandered outside and found my brother sitting on the school steps with Violet Schneider, looking at the stars.

"There's the Big Dipper," he said to her.

"Where's the big pail?" I growled. "I need a drink."

Early in October my father fulfilled his promise. We loaded my bottles from behind the lilacs onto the truck and he drove them to town and I cashed them in. Then wonder of wonders, a little more of our new prosperity trickled down to Pat and me. Father gave us each two dollars. "You might want to save it for a rainy day," he said with a smile before he turned us loose on the town.

With the money from Father and the bottle money, I now had a little over five dollars in my pocket and I was on fire. I bought comic books, chocolate bars, peanuts, pop, a hamburger, fries, and a small pearl-handled pocketknife. The result was that I had exactly eleven cents left at the end of the day, and I spent ten of them on a final black-and-white sundae. Pat went through much the same sort of joyful fling with his two dollars, except he bought some crayons and a book about bears instead of a pocketknife. Although it was an entirely wonderful day, neither one of us felt very well when we went to bed that night.

Time rolled along, and the warmth that was in the earth slowly diminished. School did not diminish, however. It went on and on, relentless and unchanging, dragging me along with it day after day, with Axel always there ready to remind me of my failures.

"Hey, Donald Duck, want to play catch today?" Or, "Hey, Donald Duck, are you gonna be a truck driver when you grow up?"

The jibes at me were always followed by ridiculing laughter from his gang. The worst part of the day, though, was the terrible longing I felt during our long lunch hour when the older boys headed for the ball field. But that would soon change.

CHAPTER TEN
Winter

One Saturday morning in November, I stood at the kitchen window and looked out at the blanket of snow that had fallen overnight. Mother stood beside me.

"I've got to milk the cow," she muttered, shivering. "I hate winter!"

As for me, I was very happy because with winter came hockey. After Mother had turned away from the window in dismay, Uncle Max's new Lincoln pulled up to the house.

"They're here!" I shouted.

"Grab your skates!" Annie cried as she rushed inside. "Everybody's down at Schneider's slough!"

Pat and I found our skates and grabbed what was left

of our hockey sticks. I had pretty well worn both of them out last winter. In fact, there was just a small bit of the heel left on mine, which made it nearly useless—hardly any better than the modified tree branches some of the kids used. Pat's hockey stick was in slightly better condition, but he refused to lend it to me anymore.

We hurriedly bundled up, then followed Annie outside to meet the winter head-on. The grown-ups stayed behind to play cards in the warm kitchen.

Out on the stoop we paused momentarily to blink at the sparkling sun, our pulses quickening as we breathed in the clean, frosty air. Pat and I stickhandled imaginary pucks with our worn-out hockey sticks as the three of us headed down the road toward Schneider's slough.

In order to create a reasonable ice-skating surface for his five daughters, and for anyone else who might care to enjoy it, every winter Mr. Schneider cleared the snow from a large area on his frozen slough. The slough was located about half a mile down the road from our lane, and the three of us had a clear view of the south end of that icy playground as we hurried toward it.

Baseball ended and hockey took over at school in the winter. I loved hockey. It had not humiliated me, and thankfully, I was a pretty fair hockey player for my age. I was at least as good as Axel, and I vowed to make myself better than him as soon as possible—much better. I would concentrate on it with all my might. At home I would spend every waking hour down at the slough. At school I'd play every day at lunch hour on the town rink.

Station Hill had a men's hockey team. Someday I'd play for them, and no one would ever look down on me again.

Word that Schneider's slough was ready for skating seemed to have been telegraphed throughout the countryside because the place was already teeming with kids. There were two distinct rinks on Schneider's slough—a hockey rink to the south and a general skating area to the north. On the south end a group of boys played hockey with a frozen horse bun, some of them using modified tree branches as hockey sticks. On the north side—separated from the hockey players by some bushes and then by a low bank of snow—a bunch of wool-clad girls, including several Schneiders, were playing crack the whip. They started by holding hands and forming a line. They would then wheel around in a great arc and send those at the end rocketing off into the snowbanks.

When I reached the rink, I could barely contain my excitement. I sat down on a packed snowbank alongside Annie and Pat, and we raced to see who would get their skates on first. It wasn't me. In fact, I didn't get my skates on at all. They simply refused to let my big feet into them, even though I discarded my heavy wool socks and tried to force them over just my thin cotton ones.

"I can't get my skates on!" I cried. But Annie and Pat were gone, already out there having fun on the ice.

I ran down the road with tears in my eyes. I didn't look back, but I could hear all the clatter and shouts ringing out behind me in the crisp winter air. Each one of them was a spike through my heart.

The grown-ups were still playing cards at the table when I burst into the kitchen.

"My skates don't fit anymore!" I cried.

"Calm down," Father said with a frown.

"Are you sure?" Mother asked worriedly.

"I tried and tried, but they wouldn't go on! Not even with just my inside socks!"

"Well then, I guess you'll just have to get some new ones," Uncle Max suggested.

"Stay out of this, Max," my father warned him.

"But I need skates!" I declared. "I need them right away! All the other kids—"

"What about the money from the bottles?" Father asked me, his eyebrows raised. "Plus the two bucks I just gave you?"

"I spent it," I confessed.

"Well then, I can't help you," he said.

"But—"

"Maybe at Christmas," he interrupted with a hard frown that stopped me cold.

I couldn't believe this was happening to me. I had to have skates. I couldn't live without them. I looked desperately to my mother for help, but she only raised her empty hands and shrugged.

"I can't wait till Christmas!" I cried.

I ran upstairs and threw myself down on the bed. It

was only November. How could I possibly survive half the winter without skates? Even if Christmas did bring relief, in the meantime Axel would be out there on the ice improving his hockey skills while I'd be standing still—not that it would matter much to me, because by then I'd have died of loneliness and boredom.

After several long hours of misery and gloom, I heard Pat and Annie come in. I didn't go downstairs to greet them. I didn't want company. In fact, I had firmly resolved to spend the rest of my life alone in the bedroom. Then Annie came upstairs. She threw herself across the bottom of the bed, emitting a huge sigh of contentment.

"Too bad your skates don't fit," she said.

"Go away," I replied.

"Are they going to buy you new ones?"

"No."

"You're going to miss all the fun! I'd die if I didn't have skates!"

Death might be a reasonable alternative for Annie, but I decided I wasn't going to give up that easily. Instead I began a determined campaign to get a new pair of skates. During the following week I alternated between desolation and outrage, lugging my huge bundle of suffering all over the house so my parents would see it every time they turned around. I whined and moaned periodically because I thought a certain amount of moaning and whining was necessary and expected. I only did the whining when Father was outside, however. He had a solid aversion to whining kids.

One day, thinking Father was outside, I once again began to whine at my mother about my lack of skates. I was just getting up steam when he came roaring into the kitchen.

"You wanted bows and arrows and you got them!" he shouted at me. "Then you had a bit of money and you wanted a knife and you got it, so you've got nothing to complain about. So stop whining about those skates—or else!"

I decided to take his advice. Anyway, I'd more than made my point with my mother, and I was convinced she was ready to buy me a pair of skates when we went into Wistola on Saturday. I knew she could afford it. She'd been saving up for an electric washing machine, but she wouldn't be buying it until after the electricity came next summer, so money was available. In the meantime, I was obliged to play hockey in my boots, like some of the others. I played on the town rink during the noon hour, slipping and sliding around the ice in my boots. It was hard to keep up with the skaters, and it seemed like whenever I managed to touch the puck, Axel would come skating out of nowhere and send me flying with a body check. I also played in my boots down at Schneider's slough. Vincent Slade was usually there waiting for a chance to skate circles around me.

Saturday finally came, and we went to Wistola as usual. However, despite my hints, there was no sign that Mother was going to do anything out of the ordinary. Eventually I gave up on subtlety and begged her outright to buy me a pair of skates.

"Aren't I as important as your electric washing machine?" I asked her.

"No," she said.

I was stunned. I looked at her with real tears in my eyes.

"Even if I wanted to, I couldn't," she said, shaking her head. "And it's your own fault. You've made your father mad with all that carrying on. If I bought them now, I'd be in big trouble."

"I want a chemistry set," Pat announced.

"Ask your father," she said with a sigh.

"Christmas is coming," she reminded me as we sped away from the city.

That night, listening at the top of the stairs, I heard them talking down below.

"I feel like an old miser," she said.

"Well, you shouldn't," he said. "He would have plenty of money of his own if he'd bothered to save it."

"I could afford to buy the skates myself," she suggested. "I could use some of my washing machine money. It's only a few dollars."

"That's not the point," he replied. "If we give in now, he'll go through life thinking all he has to do is whine and complain and he can get what he wants."

"Yes, he did carry on a bit much," she admitted. "But still... You know what it's like to be a kid."

"No, I don't," he said. "I never had a pair of skates. I can't even skate. Why, when I was his age, I was looking after three gardens on the next block, trying to help Mom out. By the time I was fifteen, I was riding the rails looking for work."

"Eddie..."

"What?"

"Don't tell me the peanuts story again," she said.

For some reason I was encouraged by their little night-time discussion. Although he might be unbending, I felt she was close to giving in.

The next day, after we returned home from lunch at Annie's, I took up my position at the window. While Mother busied herself on the other side of the kitchen I looked morosely through the frosted pane and began to suffer. She didn't seem to care. She just went about her business with nary a glance in my direction. I could have died at the window and she wouldn't have noticed. I gave up and went upstairs.

When I came downstairs a little while later, she smiled at me in a peculiar way, and I knew immediately that something was up.

"I've found a temporary solution to your skating problem," she said.

My heart jumped in my chest at her words, but when I looked in the direction she was pointing, all I saw was a pair of girls' white skates hanging from one of the coat hooks by the door.

"What?" I asked her, not understanding.

"My figure skates," she said. "You can borrow them. They'll fit you with extra socks."

"But they're girls' skates!" I cried, horrified at the idea she was proposing.

"I know, but they'll do the job for the time being," she said.

I stared bleakly at the skates. They were blindingly white, and they had long, thin silver blades with strange little sawtooth cuts at the front end. Every inch of them was female, but as I stared at them my imagination got the best of me, and I was once again gliding joyfully across the ice down at Schneider's slough. But even as I was imagining it, a whiff of fear wafted through my brain.

"I can't wear girls' skates," I said. "Everyone will think I'm a sissy."

"Well, it's the best I can do for right now," she said. "You'll get some new skates at Christmas—if you stop staring out the kitchen window."

Just then I had a brilliant idea. "I could paint them black!" I cried. "Dad's got some black paint in the dugout!"

"You'll do no such thing!" she exclaimed. "They're my figure skates!"

The expression on my face instantly changed from hope to gloom. "I'll never wear them," I vowed.

A moment later Pat came through the door in his usual happy mood. He'd always been cheerfully oblivious to my agony. He smiled at me, grabbed his skates, and headed back outside. He even began to whistle as he went out the door, and it was clear that the treacherous little rat didn't mind having fun without me. I went over to the window and watched him heading out to the road with his skates over his shoulder, and it was simply too much for me to bear. I went upstairs and collected my remnant of a hockey stick. When I returned downstairs, I put on my winter things and reluctantly lifted Mother's skates off the hook.

"Going skating?" she asked with a smile as I went out the door.

I walked down the road toward the slough, and with every step I took toward it, I became more painfully conscious of the female skates hanging from my shoulder.

Although I may have been forced to use the abominable skates, I had no intention of letting the other boys see what I had on my feet. As I neared the slough I stuck the skates under my coat and ducked into the bush. I came out at the west end of the girls' rink, where I was able to put the skates on in privacy. Fortunately, there were no boys skating on this side of the slough.

The skates did fit okay, and a moment later I was gliding around in small circles. I was in the remote western corner of the girls' side of the slough, on the north side of the rough line of low bushes that partly separated the two rinks. Where the bushes ended, a snowbank took over to complete the separation.

It was wonderful to be skating again, but I could tell that the skates hated me as much as I hated them because every now and then the sawteeth in front would deliberately catch themselves on the ice and send me on a wild forward sprawl, which usually ended with me flopping flat on the ice.

Over on the hockey rink Pat and the other boys were playing. After a while, I ventured a little beyond the edge of the bush, and from the safe side of the dividing snowbank, I looked with envy to the other side of the slough, where the hockey sticks and modified tree branches were moving the frozen horse bun back and forth between the two goals. How I wished I were with them. Then to my utter dismay and horror, I noticed that one of the few genuine hockey sticks from over there was headed my way, and attached to the end of the hockey stick was Vincent Slade. Before he could get close enough to see what was on my feet, I skated into the snowbank in order to hide the white skates on my feet from his peering eyes.

"What's wrong with you?" Vincent asked suspiciously.

"Nothing," I said, staring at him with unconcealed hostility.

"Then why are you standing in the middle of the snowbank?" he asked me.

"My feet got too hot. I'm cooling them off," I answered without hesitation.

"Yeah, but why aren't you playing hockey with the rest of us?" he asked.

"I've quit playing hockey," I replied. "I never liked it in the first place."

I delivered this amazing announcement with a convincingly defiant edge to my voice. Vincent, however, wasn't convinced.

"Are you crazy!" he exclaimed.

To this I made no reply. I had actually been feeling a

little crazy lately, but I would never admit it to someone like Vincent.

"If you hate hockey, how come you brought your hockey stick?" he asked.

While I tried to think of a decent answer to this, Vincent stared at me suspiciously, as though I were some kind of weird being from another planet. When he skated closer to me, I dug my feet deeper into the snowbank.

"I have to stay away from people," I informed him.

"Why?"

"Doctor's orders," I replied uneasily. "I've got the whooping cough." I then began to cough and whoop with tremendous gusto. He waited until my whooping frenzy subsided, then stared at me with squinting, distrustful eyes.

"If you've got whooping cough, then how come you're out here skating?" he asked.

Vincent's question was so logical that it threatened in one fell swoop to completely undo my knot of lies. In order to respond to it convincingly, I had to summon up all the ingenuity and cunning I possessed.

"The doctor said I needed to get cold air into my lungs to kill the whooping germs," I replied with hardly an instant's hesitation. I then took several deep breaths of cold air into my lungs and followed this up with a minor bout of whooping.

Vincent didn't seem to believe a word I'd said, but he finally went away. Presently I withdrew my frozen feet from the snowbank and came back onto the ice.

A parcel of girls were skating a little way down from me, but I didn't go near any of them either. However, Rachel saw me and skated over. She looked down at my white skates.

"My mother lent them to me," I said brusquely.

She smiled at me, but wisely said nothing further. "Why are you skating all by yourself?" she asked.

"Because I want to," I said irritably.

She didn't seem to mind that I was in a bad mood. She even skated with me for a while, but eventually she got lonesome for a cheerful face and returned to the girls. I went back to playing hockey quietly by myself, behind the line of bushes. I used a small piece of ice as a puck—which is not nearly as good as a frozen horse bun.

Eventually, out of sheer boredom, I became a little emboldened. I left my hockey stick behind and began to skate a bit beyond the line of bushes, where the ice was smoother. I had calculated that the snowbank would hide my white skates from any prying eyes over on the boys' side. Anyway, they were completely absorbed with their hockey game.

For a long time I continued to skate all by myself, like an ice hermit, going around and around in quiet circles. But as time went by and nothing untoward happened I grew even bolder. After deciding that the girls were unlikely to care about what kind of skates I was wearing, I skated over and joined up near the end of their whip line.

A few seconds later I was hanging on to Rachel while

the line began to move in a great circle, with the two of us at the end of it. It moved slowly at first, then with increasing speed, until it finally wheeled about and snapped, sending us flying off the end. I wound up being hurled into the snowbank, alongside Rachel.

Much to my amazement, I discovered that this simpleminded activity was fun. We laughed out loud as we brushed the snow off, then skated back and joined the line for another throw. Rachel now moved to the front of the line and I found myself at the very end of it. The end position is where the greatest force is exercised and the greatest velocity achieved.

The second time I was whipped off the end of the line, I didn't land in the snowbank. Nor did I collide with the tractor-size granite rock that stuck out of the surface of the ice over by the bushes. No, I wasn't that lucky. Instead, I was shot like a cannonball straight through the snowbank and into the clump of hockey players playing on the other side. After ricocheting off several bodies, I came to rest at the feet of Vincent Slade.

Vincent looked down at me and I saw the expression on his narrow, angular face change from surprise to puzzlement, then to disbelief, then to shock and amazement, and finally to unbridled hilarity.

"HE'S WEARING GIRLS' SKATES!" Vincent cried.

I slunk away and sat down on the snowbank next to my boots. How I wished I could crawl into those boots and stay there for the rest of my life. My already damaged reputation was now totally destroyed.

While I was taking the loathsome skates off my poor, degraded feet, Rachel skated over.

"Aren't you going to skate anymore?" she asked.

"No, I'm not," I informed her with tears in my eyes.

At least not until Christmas came and brought me a pair of skates that were the right sex.

CHAPTER ELEVEN
My Beloved Godfather

The next day at lunchtime I was back to slipping and sliding around the ice at the town rink in my boots, and I knew what was coming. As soon as Axel and his cronies had put on their skates, they whizzed past me yelling, "Hey, Donald Duck! Where're your girls' skates?" It was hard to bear, but at least it didn't last long. Hockey has a way of absorbing all your attention and all your energy.

On Tuesday there was a very special letter waiting for us at the post office. It was from my uncle Danny, the ex-baseball player and war hero who lived in Boston—the same Uncle Danny who'd sent me ten dollars last year.

"Danny isn't coming for Christmas," Mother informed us as she read the letter. "Oh my Lord! He's coming this weekend instead!"

After the excitement died down, she went back to the letter.

"He says he's anxious to see how his godson is getting along," she reported.

"Who's his godson?" I asked.

"You are. He's your godfather and you're his godson," she said. "Didn't you know that?"

I hadn't known it and I was definitely interested. "What's a godfather?" I asked her.

"Well ... It's someone who looks after the welfare of his godchild. Makes sure he's okay spiritually and otherwise. Isn't that right, honey?"

"Sounds good to me," Father said.

And it sounded good to me too. I eagerly looked forward to Uncle Danny's visit because at that particular moment I desperately needed a godfather—someone to look after me and make sure I was okay and had everything I needed to be happy, including a pair of male skates.

On Thursday night he pulled up to the house in a lean black car. He was jumped at the door by Mother and Auntie Margaret, who dragged him the rest of the way in and hugged him half to death in a huge burst of joy. Around and around the kitchen he waltzed with both Auntie Margaret and Mother in his arms at once, and the two of them couldn't get enough of him. Eventually, after things had calmed down a bit, he lifted each of us kids up in the air and kissed us. Then he shook hands with Father and Uncle Max.

"Isn't he handsome!" Annie whispered. "He looks just like Clark Gable!"

He did look a bit like Clark Gable, the famous movie star, except his eyes were too close together, his nose was wrong, and his hair was curly. But he had a mustache and a brilliant smile that was just like Clark Gable's, and he had a fresh, energetic way about him that was like Clark Gable in *Call of the Wild*.

"I wish Helen were here," Auntie Margaret said with a sigh. "Then we'd all be together."

"She could have come," Mother said in a dry voice. "She's got a railway pass, hasn't she?"

"Maybe she'll come next time," Auntie Margaret suggested.

"I saw her on my way here," Uncle Danny said. "She sends her love."

As for me, I didn't care that my other aunt hadn't come to visit us. I was happy enough just to have my beloved godfather here in my time of need.

I was standing as close as I could get to him, right beside his chair, when he suddenly turned around and took my nose between his thumb and finger. "Donald, me boy! Run out to the car and bring me the box from the backseat."

"He asked *me!*" I screamed at Annie as we raced across the snow toward the car. I got to the box first, and heavy though it was, I carried it in by myself.

The box contained a large bottle of Seagram's spirits tucked inside a purple bag. The box also contained a giant bag of chocolates, along with some books and other stuff. He threw the bag of chocolates at us kids as though it were a football.

"Eat and be merry!" He laughed as we looked in amazement at the huge bag.

"Not one," Mother said after she'd chased us into the living room and jerked the giant bag of chocolates from our hands. "Not until after supper!"

As I sat at the supper table and listened to Uncle Danny describe how he'd parachuted into France and how the French people had hidden him from the Nazis, out of the corner of my eye I watched Annie and Pat wolf down their usual vast quantities of food. As for myself—a being of superior cunning and resourcefulness—I had taken only the smallest portions of everything. No one noticed how little I was eating because of all the excitement around the table. I smiled at Annie as she shoved a huge chunk of roast beef into her open maw, then I looked down at my plate and slowly ate half a pea. I refused to touch any of the dessert, while Annie and Pat gorged themselves on hot apple pie and whipped cream.

I was amply rewarded for my calculated restraint after supper when we got the giant bag of chocolates. We took them into the living room so we could enjoy them without interference. Pat and Annie, still bloated from supper, weren't able to eat very many of them. They watched helplessly while I took over, popping a steady stream of the sweet, succulent chocolates into my mouth. Finally, when I reached the point where I couldn't swallow anymore, I noticed that the room in front of me was beginning to tilt sideways. Five minutes later I felt so dizzy and nauseated that I had to be carried upstairs and put to bed with a pail. That night I nearly died from an overdose of chocolates.

In the morning I was still too sick from acute chocolitis to go to school, but by noon I had more or less recovered. I came downstairs and found Uncle Danny and Mother talking at the table.

"How's the scout?" Uncle Danny asked.

"I feel fine," I replied. "I'm hungry."

Uncle Danny laughed and winked at me.

"He's always pulling stunts like that," Mother sighed. "Sometimes I don't know what I'm going to do with him."

"Well, I'll take him off your hands this afternoon," Uncle Danny said.

That afternoon my godfather and I drove into Wistola. On the way there he told me about the friends he wanted to see in town, and I told him in detail about the skate problem and how it was ruining my life. When I told him about the humiliation I'd suffered at the slough with the girls' skates, he burst out laughing. He stopped when he saw the expression on my face.

After having listened to my heartbreaking story, I expected him to take me directly to a store and outfit me with the best skates in town, but instead, he sent me to the afternoon movie at the Roxy while he went to visit some friends. When he picked me up outside the theater,

I fully expected our next stop would be the skate department in one of the nearby department stores.

"It's time to head back," he said, glancing at his watch.

"Back?" I said. "Can't we go to look at some skates or something?"

"No time," he said. "It's already five o'clock, and you know what your mom's like when people are late for supper."

I was so astonished that I could think of nothing to say. I just stared dejectedly out the window as my last hope of salvation disappeared behind us.

My uncle did buy me a bottle of pop when he was gassing up at the Pine Cabins Service Station, but this did nothing to ease my bitter disappointment. As a godfather, my wonderful uncle Danny had turned out to be a complete bust. I sat there in silence as he droned on about his stamp collection. What really made me angry was that he didn't notice how angry I was.

The four days of almost continuous celebration were over. Uncle Danny's suitcase was sitting by the door. His black car was warming up outside. We were saying good-bye, and the women were hanging on to him and crying their eyes out. Me, I wasn't crying. I stood next to Annie and stared coldly at the emotional scene in front of me. But then, at the very last moment, he turned to us and slapped his forehead.

"The presents!" he exclaimed. "I nearly forgot the presents!"

Presents?

They were his Christmas presents to all of us. His trunk was crammed with them. One for Annie, one for Pat, one for everybody, but especially, one for *me*!

It was a very large present, all wrapped up in brown paper with my name written on the outside.

"They should really wait until Christmas," Mother said.

"Oh, leave them alone!" said my beloved godfather with his wonderful Clark Gable smile.

It was too late anyway, for we'd already begun to rip them open and nothing short of a ten-ton gorilla could have stopped us from finishing the job.

Pat got his open first.

"What is it?" he asked.

"It's a Meccano™ set," Father informed him. "You can build things with it."

"You'll love it," my dear godfather promised him. "I had one just like it when I was a kid."

Under the brown wrapping paper that covered my present was a large box. Printed on the top of the box was a single word: SPALDING.

When I saw this strange but magical word, my heart leaped inside my chest, for I knew what was inside—a beautiful pair of Spalding skates.

My excitement was at the highest pitch in its history when I lifted the top off the box. However, my brain instantly went into reverse gear because what was inside didn't look at all like a pair of skates.

"It's a first baseman's mitt," Uncle Danny said with

his Clark Gable laugh. "I had one just like it when I was a kid."

"Before the war your uncle Danny was almost a professional ballplayer," Auntie Margaret reminded me.

"I know," I muttered as I fought back the tears.

My heart was seething with anguish and frustration as I stood in the snow with the others and waved good-bye to my godfather.

"I didn't want a stupid rag doll!" Annie cried out as soon as the rest of them had gone back inside.

"Throw it to me," I said bitterly. "I'll catch it with my first baseman's mitt."

Chapter Twelve
The Joys of Christmas

On Friday evening after my godfather had gone back to Boston, Uncle Max took Pat and me into Wistola. We ate hamburgers and fries at the White Spot, and afterward we went to the downtown arena to watch the Wistola Wings play against the Great Falls Bears. It was during that hockey game my luck suddenly began to change. It happened late in the third period when one of the referees skated over to me and put a broken hockey stick into my surprised hands.

A professional hockey stick! And it was all mine!

The next morning I set about repairing my new hockey stick. I got two pieces of wood lath from Father's little carpentry shop and layered them over the break, attaching one piece to each side of the broken staff with long rows of shingle nails. I then borrowed some of Father's heavy tape and wound it across the splints, around and around, over and over and over until the mend was about the thickness of a turkey drumstick. But I wasn't through yet. In order to make sure my new hockey stick would never wear out like the last one had, I borrowed a few hundred tacks from Father's tack tin, and I hammered them into the surface of the blade on both sides. I then covered this armor plating with several layers of tape.

All seemed to be going well. However, when I was finished with my repairs and improvements, I discovered that my hockey stick now weighed three pounds.

When I arrived at Schneider's slough, I found a scrub hockey game was in progress. A large group of kids, some with skates and some on foot like me, were all busy chasing a frozen horse bun around the rink. Into this melee I flew, pushing my armor-plated hockey stick ahead of me, and by the end of the afternoon, my formidable stick and I had made our presence felt.

I was tired, wet, and bruised when I finally had to go home for supper. Every bone in my body ached, and I felt like a walking icicle. On the positive side, I noticed that the blood from the cut above my left eye had congealed very nicely and my vision was pretty well back to normal. The winter sun, now on the far side of Charlie's hill, had dimmed considerably. But as I walked up the snow-packed road I didn't notice the approaching darkness. My heart, still burning with the thrill of exciting play, lighted my way home.

When I walked into the kitchen, Mother took one look at my bloody forehead and went white. I will not repeat here what she said to me, but by the time she was finished, I was forced to conclude that she did not understand hockey.

I continued to play hockey every day and I loved the game, but I still suffered from equipment problems. A lack of skates is a serious impediment to anyone preparing for a future in the National Hockey League. I had also entirely lost my fondness for my armor-plated hockey stick. Because it weighed three pounds, it had a tendency to resist the sudden changes in direction that are necessary when trying to stickhandle a puck. I thought of removing some of the tacks from the blade to make it lighter, but I was afraid it would fall apart when I unwrapped the tape. There was only one answer. In addition to a pair of skates, I had to get a decent hockey stick. This time I wanted a good one, not a cheap ninety-nine-cent piece of junk that would wear out in a month. I was sure my parents were going to buy me skates for Christmas, but how could I get them to buy me a hockey stick as well when they were saving every penny they had for the electricity next summer?

That night before climbing into bed, I got down on my knees and prayed fervently that God would help me get the two things I needed in order to someday make it into the National Hockey League.

Father often said that God helps those who help themselves, so before I fell asleep, I tried to think of some way to make certain both gifts showed up under the tree. I could only think of one way to do it—the direct approach. And so the next morning at breakfast I posed the question: "Could I get a good hockey stick for Christmas?" I asked them. "The one I fixed is too heavy."

"I thought you wanted skates," Mother said.

"Yeah, but I need a hockey stick too."

"Well, you're not getting both," Father said with a frown. "It's one or the other, so make up your mind."

"I want a chemistry set," Pat chirped.

"What would you do with a chemistry set?" Father asked him. "Blow us up?"

Some Christmas this is going to be, I thought. It wasn't even here yet and I was already disappointed with it. It would either be skates without a decent hockey stick or a decent hockey stick without skates. But that night before I fell asleep, a brilliant answer to my problem came to me. It involved a two-step plan.

The next day as soon as I got home from school, I started on step one. I sat down at the kitchen table and began to compose a letter. The letter was to my aunt Helen in Chicago.

We hadn't seen Aunt Helen for a long time, but she used to visit us regularly during the war, when we lived in Wistola and she lived in Portland. On the negative side she was not my favorite aunt. Whereas she doted on Annie and she loved Pat to distraction, she was able to look right at me and not see me. On the positive side she once bought me a pair of rubber boots.

Aunt Helen was married to a Union Pacific Railway station agent, so she was very wealthy. She was also the kind of person who appreciated fancy things, so I took the trouble of writing the letter in the fanciest handwriting I was capable of.

Dear Aunt Helen,

How are you? I hope you are fine. I hope Humphrey is fine too. He is my favorite dog because he is so nice. I hope Uncle Fred is fine. I hope Candice is fine too. Well, I noticed that Christmas is almost here and I was thinking about what I wanted most of all in the whole world. It was a pair of skates because my feet are size six now and my old skates don't fit me anymore. But I don't think I'll be getting any from Mother and Father. They are saving all their money for the electricity, so I'm hoping someone else who's very kind will get me what I want most of all in the whole world, which would be the best Christmas present I ever had if I could get them.

I deliberately closed my letter with "*Very, Very, Very Sincerely Yours, Donald,*" hoping that this masterly flourish, coming right at the end, would sway her to my way of thinking.

I could have asked her for the hockey stick instead of the skates, but I thought the post office would find it easier to handle a square parcel containing skates rather than an awkwardly shaped hockey stick. This is called planning for the future.

The next day at lunchtime I bought a three-cent stamp from Mrs. Zackary and mailed the letter. I was very hopeful. However, although Aunt Helen was a very educated person, having gone all the way through grade ten, she was still not entirely reliable. Last year at Christmas she'd given Pat an expensive hat with fur flaps so his ears wouldn't freeze, but all she'd given me was a book called *Captain January*, which was about a girl who lived far away in a lighthouse.

A major disappointment that was, but I wasn't the kind of person to hold a grudge for longer than a year, which was nearly up anyway. I just hoped she'd take my letter in the spirit intended and actually send me the skates for Christmas. But if she didn't, I resolved to feed a banana to Humphrey the next time I saw him.

Humphrey was Aunt Helen's Pekingese lapdog and he loved bananas. However, when he ate them, he suffered adversely. Very adversely. Until he'd recovered from their effects, he could no longer be safely held on anybody's lap nor kept in a carpeted room.

Two weeks later, with Christmas fast approaching, I received a reply from my rich aunt:

Dear Donald,

It was lovely to hear from you, although I had a little trouble reading your fancy handwriting. Perhaps you might consider printing your next letter. As to your special wish for Christmas, I think Santa has heard your request and I'm sure he'll respond favorably to it. In the meantime, don't forget to say your prayers and wash behind your ears.

With love, Aunt Helen.

My plan worked! My joy knew no bounds, and that night when supper was over, I took step two.

"I want a really good hockey stick for Christmas," I said.

"We told you before," Mother answered. "It's one or the other. We can't afford both."

"I know," I said. "But I want a hockey stick instead of the skates."

They tried to talk me out of it, but I wouldn't budge. I could have simplified things by telling them that Aunt Helen was looking after my skates, but then I would have had to explain that I'd asked her for them. I didn't think they'd like that, so I didn't tell them. As my father always said, "What you don't know won't hurt you."

"I want a chemistry set," Pat announced for the tenth time.

"You'll both get what you get," Father said in a strained voice. Talk about Christmas presents seemed to make him irritable.

"Okay, Dad," I responded amiably. "But I don't want skates. I want a hockey stick."

In the weeks that followed, my whole being was entirely

focused on the slowly approaching festive day. Then suddenly, it was just around the corner. Our Christmas tree glittered at the end of the living room, and I began to say special bedtime prayers in aid of Aunt Helen's memory. "Lord help her and guide her brain with Thy light."

By the twenty-fourth of December, my mind was fully declutched and racing in circles at a fever pitch. But I had to put on the brakes and force it down into low gear because that night I was to sing the third part of "We Three Kings" at the Christmas Eve concert in Station Hill. I enjoyed singing, and I had actually looked forward to hearing myself, but when the moment for my solo rolled around, I felt strangely depressed and nervous. I was not depressed and nervous about the singing but about whether Aunt Helen had actually followed through on my request, as promised. Well, in a few short hours I'd know the answer.

The next morning I rushed into the living room and spotted a beautiful hockey stick leaning against the wall, near the tree. And while my little brother Pat lifted the cover off his new chemistry set, I just stood there, transfixed by the sight of the stick.

Father put his hand on my shoulder and smiled. "This is a high-quality hockey stick. It'll last you for years," he said as I turned the stick over in my hands and felt the perfect heft of it. At that moment I knew that God had blessed me with the kindest, most generous father in the world—even though he was sometimes a little strict.

After thanking him for the hockey stick, I began to

ferret about the base of the tree, but I couldn't find the skates.

"What are you looking for?" Mother asked me.

"My present from Auntie Helen. I can't find it," I replied. There was a note of mild desperation in my voice.

"It's right there leaning against the wall," Father said.

"Where?" All I saw over there was a pair of skis.

"The skis," Mother said. "They're your present from Auntie Helen. She said you asked for them in a letter. Don't you remember?"

"Skis!" I cried. "I asked for skates!"

"In this world you don't always get what you want," Father remarked.

"But I didn't ask for skis! I hate skiing! I don't even know how to ski."

"Now, don't be ungrateful," Mother said. "Those skis cost a lot of money."

"Look at all these chemical things," Pat said, displaying the contents of his new chemistry set.

I glanced at the array of diminutive jars containing the chemicals and wondered absently if maybe there was something in there that might end my misery.

"These are top-quality skis," Father said calmly, turning them over in his hands. "Look at this," he said. "Made from genuine hickory wood. They'll last a lifetime."

I was extremely unhappy with the way things had turned out, but at least I had my beautiful new hockey stick. That was something, and an hour later I headed down to Schneider's slough to try it out. In my Christmas stocking I'd gotten a new puck to go with my stick, and although I still felt a sting of disappointment over the skates, I knew I had nothing to complain about.

Little Larry Altinkinker was alone on the ice when I arrived, and that was fine with me. I stickhandled my new puck past him again and again, and he was unable to do anything about it. I had the talent, and with my new, lighter hockey stick I was unstoppable—until he accidentally stopped me. Rather he stopped my hockey puck when I was on the way past him, and he shot it like a bullet into the snowbank at the edge of the rink.

I would have killed him on the spot, but he had a big brother who wrestled steers, so I gave him a powerful tongue-lashing instead. Unfortunately, while I was shouting at him I lost track of exactly where it was my puck had disappeared into the snowbank. We searched for it for over half an hour, but without success.

In the meantime, others had arrived at the rink and a fierce hockey game was now under way. Energized as I was, partly by anger and frustration, and partly by my new hockey stick, I plunged into it like a Tasmanian devil. Within seconds my anger had vanished and I was totally immersed in the game. With or without skates, this is what I was meant to do in life. I was sure of it.

Later on, while I was sitting on the snowbank catching my breath, Big Herman Dubrowski came by and picked up my stick. Big Herman had been kicked out of high school last year because he liked to beat people up.

"It's my new hockey stick," I said with tears in my eyes.

"I'm just going to borrow it for a second," he replied gruffly.

What could I do? Nothing. And so for the next ten minutes, I watched in agony as my new hockey stick played hockey without me.

Finally Big Herman threw my hockey stick onto the snowbank beside me, then he climbed on his horse and rode away. I breathed a heavy sigh of relief and headed back to the hockey game. But before I reached it, I made a heart-stopping, gut-wrenching discovery. The blade on my beautiful, brand-new hockey stick was cracked across the middle, from one end to the other. In fact, there was little, if anything, to hold it together—as I discovered when it fell apart. The cry I let out brought everyone on the rink to a dead stop.

"It's broke!!" I screamed. "It's busted!"

Tears were running down my face and fear was cartwheeling around in my heart as I plodded toward home. I would have to tell Father about the stick immediately because I knew it would be much worse for me if he discovered it for himself. When I came into the kitchen, he looked at me and smiled.

"How's the new hockey stick?" he asked.

"It's broken," I murmured sadly. Father stared dumbly at me for a split second, then erupted.

"Broken? Broken! How can it be broken? It's brand-new!!"

I explained rapidly what had happened, but it didn't help. It only made him more furious.

"I'm sorry," I said dejectedly.

"Well, at least you've still got your new puck," Mother said.

"No I haven't," I said glumly. "I lost it in the snowbank."

"What!" Father cried. "You what?"

"Eddie," Mother broke in, "don't be too hard on him. He's feeling bad enough as it is. And it's Christmas, after all."

"Christmas!" Father roared. "I'll Christmas him on his backside!"

"You'll do nothing of the sort unless you want a real fight on your hands," Mother said. "Now sit down and cool off!"

Instead of sitting down, Father drew himself up to his full height. Carefully controlling his rage, he turned to me. "I'll tell you one thing," he said. "You're not going to lay your mitts on those skis until you've learned to look after things."

That was fine with me. I didn't want them in the first place. In fact, I hated them.

"Now, that is ridiculous!" Mother responded angrily. "They're his skis. Helen gave them to him, and you've got no right to take them away."

"He's my son!" Father said angrily. "I'll do what I please with him!"

"Then you can do what you please with Christmas dinner because I'm not cooking it," Mother responded, taking off her apron and throwing it at him. "I suggest you start by basting the turkey."

"Baste the turkey!" Father cried. "I'll throw the blasted thing out in the snow and kick it over the barn!"

"Go ahead," Mother said. "And when Max and Margaret get here looking for their Christmas dinner, you can feed them cranberry sauce!"

"Please don't fight," Pat interjected. "You're scaring my kitty."

In the end Mother won the argument. Or so it seemed to me because when the shouting finally subsided into angry silence and she put her apron back on, there was just a hint of a smile in the way she looked at me.

"All right, Donald," she said. "It's okay for you to go."

"Go where?" I asked.

"Go skiing," she said. "What do you think we've been arguing about?"

"But I don't want to go skiing," I protested.

She then leveled her eyes at me, and they were like two black cannons ready to discharge their shot.

"Go and ski," she hissed.

Unfortunately, there was no shortage of hills in our vicinity. About half a mile north of Charlie's, there was a part of the hill that kids tobogganed down, most of them using chunks of cardboard instead of toboggans. It was called Suicide Hill, and I plodded toward it, my skis over my shoulder, my poles in hand, and my heart thoroughly pitted by the worm of despair.

Suicide Hill consisted of two sections, a steep upper section and an easier lower one. The two sections were separated by a narrow path about halfway up. When I got there, I discovered a pack of tiny kids busy sliding down the lower slope. Evidently, they'd never seen skis before, and they quickly gathered around me. When I told them what I was going to do, they didn't believe me. In fact, I scarcely believed it myself.

I climbed up the hill with leaden feet, followed by the mob of tiny kids. I stopped at the top of the lower slope and went along the path a little way to a slightly wider section where most of the downhill sliding activity began. Once there, I put my skis on, took my poles in my hands, and managed to point myself downhill. I then began to move in a downward direction, traveling at top speed for a total distance of about five feet before I went head over heels.

After I'd dug my head out of the snow, I heard laughter and hoots of derision from the multitude of tiny kids on the sidelines. This made me downright angry, and I vowed not to leave the accursed hill until I'd gone down it in an upright position.

After a couple of hours of falling down the lower slope, it seemed to me that I was improving. And during the struggle I'd made a significant discovery. It was fun. I began to wonder absently if there might be a future for me in the sport of skiing.

"Why don't you go all the way down from the top?" one of the tiny multitude of observers suggested as I trudged up the hill for the hundredth time.

I looked up at the top of the hill. It was a very long distance away, and the top half of the hill was much steeper than the gentle bottom slope. On the other hand, a little way over to my left there was a clear run with unpacked snow all the way from the top to the bottom, and it occurred to me that skiing all the way down from the very top would be an impressively brave way to end the afternoon. Even if I didn't quite make it, word of my brave attempt would soon get around, and it might help to restore my sullied reputation. And if I did happen to make it all the way down without falling, my feat would live forever in the memories of this multitude of tiny witnesses.

But was it safe? I was sure it was. At that time I was of the fixed opinion that it's impossible to really hurt yourself falling in the snow. After all, I'd already done it a hundred times so far this morning and I was still walking upright.

I reached the top after a long and difficult ascent, second only to scaling Mount Everest on its bad side. Once there, I sat down in the snow and rested. A few minutes later I stood up, put on my skis, and clenched the ski poles firmly in my mittened hands. I then inched my way to the edge of the hill.

When I looked down, I finally understood why they called it Suicide Hill. *I'm going to get killed,* I thought. On the other hand, it was going to be difficult for me to back out at this late date, for I now had a large audience of spectators scattered about the hill, all waiting impatiently for me to commit suicide.

While I was wondering how to extricate myself from the situation, I happened to move my skis slightly and my problem was solved. I was on my way down. Faster and faster I went, faster and faster, down, down, down the hill. And suddenly, it looked like I might actually do it! But then I noticed a large lump of snow directly ahead of me, and not knowing how to turn, I couldn't avoid it.

The lump of snow was very hard, very substantial, and the next thing I knew, I was cartwheeling through the air like a cow in a tornado.

When I opened my eyes, I saw several skis poking up through the snow in front of me. Like the miracle of the loaves and the fishes, my skis had multiplied before my eyes. But a moment later I realized there had not been a miracle on Suicide Hill, after all. My skis had not multiplied. When all the pieces were added up, there was still only one pair.

Yes, my brand-new skis from Chicago were smashed to smithereens, and it was all Aunt Helen's fault for not being able to read my handwriting.

A few minutes later I limped back up to the lump of snow and discovered it was not a lump of snow at all but rather a large granite boulder that Satan had installed on the surface of the hill in order to kill kids on skis.

A half hour later when my thumping heart and the rest of me entered the warm kitchen, I observed, as in a dream, my mother basting the turkey. Pat was nowhere in sight, but Father was there. He was sitting at the corner of the table, staring morosely out the window.

I steeled myself for the slaughter, and in a trembling voice, I made my announcement.

"I skied all the way down Suicide Hill," I said.

"That's nice," Mother replied.

"But I hit a big rock," I said.

"Oh?" she responded. "You didn't hurt yourself?"

Now it had to come. I looked at him and I began to tremble.

"No, but I broke my skis."

"Oh no!" Mother exclaimed. "Not your new skis!"

I heard her well enough, but my eyes did not move from him. Yet he only kept on staring out the window. His head did not turn, not even a fraction of an inch. Didn't he hear what I'd said?

"Yeah," I said in a quaking voice, "I really busted them up. There's five pieces altogether."

Still the figure by the window did not move or speak.

"Dad?" I said.

"I heard you," he replied in a distant voice. "Too bad."

That was it? Just "too bad"?

"What's wrong with Dad?" I whispered.

"Don't bother him right now," Mother whispered back. "He's still recovering from the explosion."

"What explosion?" I asked in a mystified voice.

"Pat blew up your bedroom with his chemistry set," she informed me.

"Blew it up? Is he dead?"

"No," Father said. "Unfortunately."

"He was very lucky," Mother said. "He just got a little burn on his arm."

"Blew it up?" I repeated.

"He certainly did," she said. "There was a loud BOOM—like thunder, only a little louder—and the whole house shook. Scared me half to death, and when we ran upstairs, the room was on fire. Your dad had to use a blanket to put it out."

After contemplating this startling information for a few seconds, its full implication hit me like a sledgehammer.

"My comic books!" I cried.

Fortunately, my precious comic books were not injured. They were in a corner of the bedroom that had escaped the conflagration. The bedroom curtains, however, were not so lucky. Only burned scraps of them remained, making a curiously interesting fringe across the top of the window. Our bed was still damp from the water thrown at it. It had been singed a bit, but was otherwise intact. However, the old card table, which had evidently been the site of the chemical experiment, had not fared so well. A large crater had been blasted through the middle of it, and its remaining surface was thoroughly stained with the ghastly, multicolored residue of chemicals gone awry.

Pat himself had a bandage on his arm, which he proudly displayed to me. Except for taking obvious pride in the explosion he'd created, he was otherwise completely unaffected by the disaster. In fact, it seemed to me that he would have liked to repeat the experiment—and he might have done so, had his chemistry set not been totally destroyed in the explosion.

"You shoulda seen it!" he exclaimed, his eyes wide with excitement. "I just mixed a bunch of the chemical stuff with some shoe polish and I lighted this match and BOOM!"

"I broke my skis," I informed him in response.

But he didn't seem to hear me. His eyes were all aglow, and his mind was far away—farther away than normal.

"I'm going to be a scientist when I grow up," he announced in a grave voice.

"And blow up the world?" I asked.

Later in the day after being advised that he was never to touch a match without permission, Pat was released from his bedroom prison. After the table was set and everything was ready for Christmas dinner, he reported from the window that Uncle Max's new Lincoln had just stopped in front of the house. I paid little attention because I was busy thinking that I had nothing left to live for. All I had was an archery set I'd lost interest in, a lost puck, a broken hockey stick, and pieces of skis made in Chicago.

"They've brought presents!" Pat cried from the window.

Their presents were as wonderful as they were unexpected. Topping everything else, I got a brand-new pair of male skates. I was so overwhelmed with joy that I couldn't speak for ten minutes.

The others fared equally well. Mother got a lovely set of hand-embroidered tea towels, and Father got a nice pair of leather work gloves.

As for Pat, they gave him a large, deluxe-model, seventy-four-piece All-Star Chemistry Set.

Highlighted by a very well basted turkey, Christmas dinner was wonderful. While we ate and laughed and talked, slowly but surely Father returned to normal.

Toward the end of the meal, I told our relatives about

my experience that afternoon on Suicide Hill and how thoroughly I'd broken Aunt Helen's skis. For some reason Uncle Max seemed to think the whole thing was funny. I personally didn't think so, but I laughed to keep him company because I now loved him.

CHAPTER THIRTEEN
Thunder

Early in January, Mother bought me a new hockey stick before Father was able to forbid it, and I spent most of my free time in hockey heaven. Then March came along—much too soon—and sadly, hockey was back on the shelf for another year.

As soon as the field behind the school was dry enough, baseball started again. I missed baseball terribly, but I had sworn never to play again and I never went back on my word. I mostly passed the time reading. I'd read all the Hardy Boys books twice—all that the Wistola Library had—but since then, I'd discovered some humorous books by a writer named Robert Benchley, and I was slowly making my way through them. I enjoyed them a lot, but reading books wasn't enough.

On the positive side, the memory of my humiliation in the game with Melody had faded somewhat over the winter. But with the start of baseball, a sneering taunt from Axel brought it all back. I had just come outside at lunchtime when I ran into him.

"Hey, Donald Duck! Gonna play baseball with us, or are you afraid you might get hit by another beanball?" he asked.

"I told you before," I said. "I'm not playing anymore."

"But how are you going to make it to the big leagues like Uncle Danny if you don't practice?" he asked with a grin.

"My uncle never played in the big leagues," I replied impatiently for the hundredth time. "He joined the Army Air Force instead." Although I could feel my blood pressure rising, I managed to speak calmly.

"So you ain't gonna play no mo', no mo'?" he said in a singsong voice.

I gave him a hard look, then turned away.

I hated Axel with all my heart. I hated the sound of his voice. I hated his face. I hated his easygoing self-confidence. But what I hated most of all was the feeling of inferiority I had when I was around him.

"He's going to play volleyball with the girls," I heard Vincent Slade say as I walked away from them.

"Can't you think of a new joke, Slade," I yelled back angrily.

Later that day after I'd come home from school, I was looking wearily out the kitchen window and wishing with all my heart that God would make something interesting happen, just to relieve the monotony. Something. Anything. *Life in the city is a lot more interesting,* I thought. *Things happen in the city.*

A moment later, while I was still at the window, Dad came back from looking over the fields and he tripped coming up the steps. It was about the most exciting thing I'd seen all week.

"Thanks, God, but it's not enough," I said.

I sometimes talked to God like that, but it was just kind of a personal joke. I knew that God doesn't respond to silly wishes. The fact that Father happened to trip on the steps just as I asked God to relieve the boredom around here was simply a coincidence.

He wasn't hurt at all except for a banged knee. He came inside rubbing it.

"How does it look?" Mother asked him.

"It's coming along," he replied.

"Sally Klappstein came by while you were out there," she informed him as he headed for the washbasin. "She said there's a traveling evangelist coming to the church on Sunday. The Reverend Ronald Kluny. She says he's quite famous for his preaching."

"Good. We'll go in and take a look at him," he said.

I'd never heard of a traveling evangelist, and I thought it would be interesting to see what he was like. It might help relieve the boredom. But when Sunday came, rain was bucketing down out of a black sky and there was lightning and thunder all around us.

"I guess we won't be going anywhere today," Mother said with a sigh. "The section road will be awful. We'll never get out."

"But we have to go!" I cried.

"I've never known you to be that interested in church," Mother said. "Are you feeling all right?"

"I just want to see the traveling evangelist," I explained.

"I want to see him too," Pat piped up.

"Well, maybe we'll give it a try," Father said.

"What about Goldie?" Mother asked with a worried look.

Goldie was our cow, and she was expecting a calf.

"She'll be fine," he said. "Max said it won't happen for a couple of weeks."

"Are you sure we should go?" she asked. "The road will be awful."

"We'll make it," Father promised.

I knew and Mother knew, and even Pat knew, that Dad enjoyed driving our one-ton truck over bad roads. A deep mud puddle or a mountainous snowdrift was a personal challenge for him, and he loved to get the old truck up to top speed and plow through such obstacles. Mother didn't actually care too much for this sort of adventure, but Pat and I liked it a lot. Besides, Father worked very hard, so he deserved to have a little fun.

"I've got a bad feeling about this," Mother said later, as we ducked through the rain and climbed into the truck.

We chugged out to the end of our lane and stopped there to assess the situation. The section road was far worse than I'd ever seen it before. There were deep puddles everywhere, on both sides of the little creek bridge. All this made Father very happy, but as I sat there in the rumbling truck and stared at the flooded road I seriously doubted that we'd get ten feet before we bogged down. Father, however, had no such reservations. He shifted into reverse, backed up a little way, and stopped. He smiled happily, shifted into low, and we were off. He quickly shifted into second gear, giving it all the gas it would take, then he drove the old truck at high speed straight into the muddy obstacle course.

We had Lady Luck on our side. Hurtling into the muck like an amphibious beast from the prehistoric past, the old one-ton sloshed and slithered its way through everything. We even made it past the low spot alongside Schneider's slough. At the end of the section road, we turned onto the somewhat safer graveled road that went south to Station Hill.

"Nothing to it!" Father laughed as chains of yellow lightning electrified the sky all around us.

I couldn't remember ever seeing the little church in Station Hill so dark inside. Even the six coal oil lamps along the walls did little to lift the interior gloom. Outside it was almost as dim and murky as it was inside the church—except when the fierce incandescence in the sky lit up the earth. In between the flashes, when everything was dark and gloomy again, I had to remind myself it was only ten o'clock in the morning.

There was another flash of lightning, followed by an almighty clap of thunder that shook the little building right down to its rubblestone foundation. At the same instant up at the front of the church, the famous evangelist appeared on this side of the yellow door. He did not resemble the Reverend Hittle in any way. He was a big, wide-shouldered, powerful man, with craggy features and unruly black hair. His tangled black eyebrows were grown together in a thick, continuous mat. But it was his eyes that caught our attention. Their glance was fierce and hot, like those of an angry badger. They burned into us when he looked our way.

A tall, elderly lady with short gray hair and hard, cold eyes came in behind him. She wore a black gown and a high white collar with a wooden crucifix fastened at the front of it. She carried a large Bible in her hands.

The sermon that the Reverend Kluny gave us was completely unlike anything the Reverend Hittle had ever served up. Instead of talking about heaven, the fierce evangelist told us about hell. And he let us have it with both barrels. Indeed, he gave us such a horrific vision of the awful things that reigned down below that, at the height of his frenzy, I thought I could hear dark wings thumping against the floor under my feet.

"Evil is around us!" he roared, his eyes flaming up like

the lightning outside. "Beware, O sinners! Beware! Lucifer is coming!"

"He is coming!" echoed the lady in black, and the sound of her thin, high-pitched voice sent a shiver up my spine.

"He frightened me," Mother said afterward as we slithered down the road toward Cousin Annie's.

"She scared me worse," I confessed.

"Me too," Pat chimed in.

"It was a good one, all right," Father happily admitted. "Worth every penny."

A huge lunch was waiting for us in Auntie Margaret's warm kitchen, and we were soon sitting comfortably around her big wooden table.

"That evangelist this morning was a hot one," Father said with a smile. "Hell and damnation. He really gave it to us!"

"Hell and all that nonsense, eh?" Uncle Max laughed, contentedly patting his magnificent potbelly.

"Yeah," Father replied. "It was something. Hell and Lucifer. 'Lucifer's coming,' he said. And he sounded like he really believed it too!"

"Do you believe it?" Uncle Max asked, his eyes narrowing as they always did when he was about to start an argument with our father.

"Well, I guess I have to believe in Lucifer if I believe in God," Father replied. "But I don't think Mister Lucifer's going to pay us a personal visit," he added with a laugh.

"It's all nonsense," Uncle Max said disdainfully.

"If he does come, I know the soul he's going to collect first," Father said sourly.

"Now, don't you two start," Mother intervened. "We've had enough religion for one day."

After Mother's warning, everyone settled down and devoted their attention to the lunch until Pat looked across the table with a puzzled expression on his face.

"Who's Lucifer?" he asked.

It was as though he'd spent the entire morning somewhere else.

Father smiled at him. "He's the devil," he said. "Satan. The Evil One."

Pat nodded and everyone began to eat again. Except for Uncle Max. He placed his fork down on his plate, patted his lips with his napkin, and smiled across the table at Dad.

"Actually, he isn't, you know," he said in his best high-school-graduate voice.

"Yes he is," Father replied, casually spearing a big fat pickle with his fork.

"I'm afraid not," Uncle Max said with a superior smile.

"Who is he, then?" Father asked, his brow creasing in annoyance as he bit the end off the pickle.

"Lucifer is one of the archangels." Uncle Max smiled. "Was, I mean. He fought on the devil's side when the devil challenged God, but he's not actually the devil. Not that I believe a word of it," he concluded. He picked up his fork and began to eat again, content that he'd set Dad straight.

Father speared a piece of cold roast beef and stuck it in his mouth. After chewing in silence for a minute, he put his fork on his plate and stared at Uncle Max. "Then who's Satan?" he demanded to know.

Uncle Max quietly put his fork down on his plate and patted his lips with his blue napkin. "Satan was an archangel too. He also went with the devil. There's Lucifer, there's Satan, and there's the devil, but they're three different beings. In the story, I mean. If you want to believe it."

"That's wrong," Father responded with determination. "You're just making it up as you go along. Satan is Lucifer and Lucifer is the devil. They're all the same person—or whatever you call them."

"Neither one of you knows what you're talking about," Mother commented.

"I do. He doesn't," Father said.

"Ha!" said Uncle Max.

"I just wish everybody would stop talking about him," Auntie Margaret said with a worried frown.

"He comes if you talk about him," Annie volunteered in a strange, quavering voice. Following this startling pronouncement, she turned her eyes up into their sockets, so only the whites showed. Then she screwed up her face and hung her tongue out of her mouth in a remarkably apt depiction of what the devil might indeed look like if he cared to pay us a visit.

"Annie, stop making that awful face and eat your lunch," Auntie Margaret said nervously.

Father and Uncle Max put their forks down and stared hard across the table at each other.

Uncle Max spoke first. "Well, I can't help it if you're wrong," he said with a stony smile.

Father stared at him even harder, and everyone paused in their eating to watch the contest of wills.

"Stop it, Edward," Mother said. "You're spoiling our lunch."

"He started it," Father declared, still staring at Uncle Max.

"Well, a fact is a fact," Uncle Max said. "They're three different things."

"There's pumpkin pie for dessert," Auntie Margaret interjected with a worried look.

"Go get your Bible," Father said in an ominous tone of voice. "It's written in there."

"I haven't got a Bible," Uncle Max said.

"I might have known," Father said with a grim smile.

"Edward!" Mother said.

There was a long moment of silence, then Auntie Margaret stood up and fluttered her hands at the men.

"I'll get the pumpkin pie," she said.

As soon as Auntie Margaret went out, Pat looked up the table at Father.

"Where does Lucifer live?" he asked.

"Don't say it," Mother said to Father.

"Nearby," Father said, looking straight at Uncle Max.

Uncle Max now had a strained, angry look on his face. He was struggling to come up with a good reply, but he couldn't think of one. It was just then that Auntie Margaret came running back into the room with an expression of extreme distress on her big round face.

"I've lost my pumpkin pie!" she exclaimed.

"What do you mean, you've lost your pumpkin pie!" Uncle Max scoffed. "Don't be ridiculous!"

"But it's gone!" Auntie Margaret cried. "I put it on the cooling shelf on the porch and now it's gone!"

"It can't be gone." Uncle Max frowned. "You must have put it somewhere else."

"But I didn't," Auntie Margaret protested. "I put it right there on the shelf after I baked it this morning. I know I did."

"You're being silly, Margaret. Who would take a pie from inside our back porch?" Uncle Max asked her. Then he looked at Annie and his eyes narrowed.

"I didn't take it!" Annie protested.

"She wouldn't," Auntie Margaret affirmed.

"Well then, where's the pie?" Uncle Max demanded.

"I don't know!" Auntie Margaret cried, wringing her hands in anguished bewilderment.

Before long, everyone was searching for Auntie Margaret's pie, but it had indeed vanished without a trace. We even looked in the oven, just in case she had forgotten to take it out, but it wasn't in there either. Then Uncle Max accused Auntie Margaret of only imagining she'd baked a pie, and Auntie Margaret burst into tears and ran into the bedroom.

It was as if some kind of shadow had descended on the

old farmhouse and made everybody angry at everybody else. Father and Uncle Max were still mad at each other over the Lucifer argument, and Mother was mad at Uncle Max for accusing Auntie Margaret of not baking a pie. In fact, everyone seemed to be mad at Uncle Max, and in addition, Mother was mad at Father. Even we kids got into the act. I got mad at Annie for cheating at Chutes and Ladders, and she got mad at me for catching her at it. Then Pat became mad at both of us when we counted wrong and sent him down a long chute.

The only one there who wasn't mad at anyone was Auntie Margaret, who had come out of the bedroom and gone back to searching for her pie.

"It was my Eleanor Roosevelt pie pan," she moaned. "It had her head engraved on the bottom! Ohhh! I'll never have another one like it!"

It was dark by the time we left for home. The pie—and the Eleanor Roosevelt pie pan that contained it—were never found, and everyone was still in a bad mood. Only the heavens had improved. The storm was gone. Clouds still obscured much of the sky, but now and then we had a glimpse of the moon.

As we skidded along the slimy roads toward home Father looked over at Mother and tried to smile.

"It's quit raining," he declared.

"I noticed," Mother replied, without looking at him.

"Funny about that pie," he said.

"I don't want to discuss it," she responded in a voice that was as dry as the Sahara.

"Well, I didn't take it!" Father said with sudden anger.

We had been spinning along the graveled north-south road, barreling through puddles at top speed. We turned the corner onto our section road, and we managed to slither down to Schneider's big white house without serious incident. However, after going a little farther down the road, the headlights revealed a major obstacle directly in front of us. Father hit the brakes and we slid to a squishy stop.

Schneider's slough had grown appreciably during our absence. It was now a huge black lake that extended across the road from field to field and down the road for at least fifty yards.

"Don't even think about it," Mother warned him.

We all expected Father would drive us back to Cousin Annie's for the night, which would have been the logical way to handle the situation. We certainly didn't expect him to do what he did. What he did was back the truck up for twenty feet, shift it into low, and accelerate straight at the huge lake in front of us.

"Edward!" Mother cried. "Are you crazy!"

"It's not deep," he grunted as the truck roared into the black lake, splashing great sheets of water to the sides.

We came to an oozing stop about thirty feet into it, and there we stayed, despite Father's best attempts to rock us out. At last he turned off the motor and shook his head. "That was stupid," he said.

Mother said nothing.

"Are we going to drown?" Pat asked.

"Of course not," Mother replied calmly. "Your father will get us out of this mess. Won't you, darling?"

"We're going to have to wade through it to get home," he said uneasily.

"Are we going to drown?" Pat asked again.

"No, we're not going to drown," Father said irritably.

"Oh Lord," Mother moaned. "And us in our Sunday clothes!"

"Can't be helped," he said glumly.

"Yes it can," she said. "Take off your shoes and socks and your pants and shirts. Leave them up on the seat when you get out."

"Why?" Pat asked.

"So they won't be ruined," she said. "Now get busy."

It was extremely congested inside that truck for the next few minutes as we struggled to undress without getting a bloody nose from all the swinging elbows. But we finally made it.

Father used a match to light the trouble lantern, then we gingerly stepped out of the truck and into the water. It wasn't really very deep, just a few inches below the door of the truck. At first the water was freezing cold, but it began to feel warmer as our feet and legs grew numb.

We picked our way carefully around to the front of the vehicle, as instructed. The mud sucked at our feet as we went forward. Father held the lantern high, and we looked out at the expanse of black water that seemed to recede forever into the darkness.

"We could pretend we're going for a swim," I suggested.

"Let's hope to heaven it doesn't come to that," Mother said grimly.

"Stay right behind me, and keep in a straight line," Father warned us. "I mean it," he said emphatically. "Don't stray out of line, because there's the ditch on both sides of the road and you could drown in it."

"I'll go last," Mother said. "I'll watch them."

We were on our way, with Pat and me following closely behind Father, the three of us in our long underwear. At the end of the line, Mother followed in her petticoat.

For some distance across the shallow lake, everyone was silent, then I heard a low chuckle behind me. When Father looked back, Mother laughed out loud.

"You look like the lead duck," she giggled.

"Just watch where you're going," Father cautioned, still looking back at us. "Remember, there's a ditch on either side of the road."

While he was still looking back at us Father managed to locate the ditch, and he disappeared under the water. Our light went down with him and we were plunged into darkness.

"Edward!" Mother cried out.

"Don't move!" a voice spluttered. "I'm all right. Just stay where you are!"

At that very instant the moon came out from behind a cloud. It shone down on the water, lending a tropical, romantic atmosphere to the scene, and I saw our father rise from the black sea like Neptune. He shook his head and wheezed.

Mother burst out laughing, and so did Pat and I. In fact, Dad was the only one there who was able to contain himself.

"I've lost the lantern," he gasped. "We'd better make tracks and get across the rest of this before the moon disappears again."

"I'm cold," Pat announced between chattering teeth.

"Me too," I echoed.

"We'll be home in a few minutes," Mother assured us as we slogged through the water.

Presently the four of us emerged from the Schneiders' new lake and started down the last stretch of muddy road toward our lane. It wasn't long before I began to recognize the trees along the side, and finally, I saw the dark outline of our roof against the sky. And then Bounce came barking out toward us, welcoming us back.

Once we were inside the house, we washed off the mud, dried ourselves, and changed into our pajamas. We were soon huddled around our big kitchen stove, sipping hot cocoa as the bone-chilling cold turned into glorious warmth. But Father was still shivering.

"Oh Lord, I hope you don't get pneumonia again," Mother sighed.

Last year Father had come down with pneumonia after he'd rescued the Reverend Hittle in a snowstorm.

"Right about now I could sure use a sip of brandy," he responded.

"There's that unopened bottle of rye Danny gave

you," she pointed out. "Maybe I should give you a drink of that."

"No," Father said with determination. "That's twelve-year-old bonded premium whiskey. I'm saving it for a special occasion."

As I drank my second cup of cocoa I remembered the lady in black. A shiver went down my spine, and I thanked heaven she wasn't my mother.

"I'll take the tractor down and pull the truck out tomorrow," Father declared.

"I'll help you," I volunteered.

"Sure," he said with a nod at me. "You can steer it when I pull her out."

"At least we didn't ruin our good clothes," Mother said reflectively. "Imagine having to replace them."

"We wouldn't have," he responded. "Just clean them up, that's all."

"They'd never be the same," she interrupted, shaking her head, "and I won't have us shabby."

"Who said anything about being shabby?" he asked in an irritated voice.

"They would look shabby," she insisted.

"You kids can find the lantern when the ditch dries up," he said, changing the subject.

Mother held her cup up to her lips with both hands and sipped her cocoa. "It's been a very strange day," she said. "First that preacher and that horrible thunderstorm, and then...all these things. Margaret's pie disappearing, and all that arguing about the devil. Then the road flooded like that and us wading across it. It's all so—"

"What are you talking about?" Father asked her.

"I don't know. I just feel a little uneasy. I feel like something else is going to happen."

"What's going to happen?" I asked.

"Never mind," she said, standing up. "Anyway, it's time you two were in bed."

She lit the small lamp and put it in my hands. I moaned a little in protest because I was quite warm and comfortable where I was.

At that exact moment my little brother was stricken with a thought. "Who comes?" he asked.

"What are you talking about?" Mother asked.

"Annie said 'he comes' when you talk about him. Who comes?"

"Never mind. It's just a lot of nonsense," she said. "Now off you go to bed. It's been a long day."

As we walked across the living room floor I leaned toward Pat and whispered, "Lucifer comes."

While I was leading the way up the stairs with the lamp in my hand, I looked back and saw our shadows climbing up the wall behind us. But between the two shadows I thought I saw a third shadow—the shadow of a head, with two horns protruding from it. I stopped dead in my tracks, and the lamp trembled in my hand. The shadow was instantly gone, but it had been there. I was sure of it.

"What's wrong?" Pat asked me.

"I'm going back down," I said. In fact, I was already

past him, heading down the stairs. But even though I had a head start, Pat still managed to reach the bottom of the stairs before I did. Not having a lamp to contend with, he could move faster.

We made it to the kitchen intact, and I told them about the shadow I'd seen on the stairs—a shadow with horns. Pat backed me up all the way, even though he hadn't seen a thing. After listening to our story, Father promptly turned us around and sent us on our way—back upstairs. Bounce came with us for protection; however, he sensed something was up and he refused to set a paw on the stairs until we were at the top and he saw it was safe. And even then we had to coax him up. A minute later Pat and I were in bed, our bodies shielded from strange shadows and other ghastly things by our dead grandmother's quilt, which we took out of the cedar chest for this occasion. It was about ten times as heavy as any other quilt in our house, but it was very warm. We only used it on extremely cold nights because after a night under Grandma's quilt, we felt like a pair of pressed flowers in the morning. However, on the positive side, it was the next best thing to being protected by a layer of solid lead. We also had our fearless guard dog to protect us. Down at the bottom of the bed, he was already muttering his way to sleep.

Moonlight streamed in through the window. Part of it struck the old card table, and the rest of it lay gently across the edge of our bed. A cool night breeze billowed the curtains while noises from the next room informed us that Mother and Father were upstairs and getting ready for bed. Now, at last, I felt perfectly safe. I closed my eyes with the wish that I would always be as warm and secure as I felt just then, even though I knew I'd be compressed to the thickness of a doormat by the time morning rolled around.

"What's that?" Pat whispered.

I had heard nothing, but I seized upon the opportunity.

"It's him," I said, going rigid and staring at the window.

"Who?" Pat asked.

"Lucifer," I said. "He's coming to get you."

In short order Pat was reduced to a quivering lump, deep under Grandma's quilt. I smiled at the lump, then I absently turned my gaze back to the window. And that's when I heard the noise. It was a scratching sound from outside, like the sound of an animal clawing for purchase on the porch roof, below our window. Bounce leaped from the bottom of our bed and scrambled under it. And then before I had a chance to join Pat under the covers, a black form hurtled through the open window and into our room.

I screamed. Pat screamed under the covers. Bounce yelped with fright from under the bed.

"I'm coming!" Father shouted from the next room. A second later he plunged into our room, but by then I had made an important discovery.

"It's okay, Dad." I laughed. "It's only Cannibal."

Cannibal was our cat, and he posed no danger to anyone—although the ghosts of the mice that had passed through him might say otherwise.

Father went over to the window. He leaned on the sill, looking outside in silence.

"I thought it was Lucifer," I explained.

"It's been a long day," he said at last. "And there's been too much silliness all 'round. Now listen carefully—because I'm only going to say this once. If there is a Lucifer, this is the last place on earth he'd come to. He likes cities because that's where the serious sinning is done. Now go to sleep!"

He's right, I thought. *If Lucifer ever did make it out here, he'd soon be bored out of his evil mind.*

Later, after Father had gone away, I looked over at Pat. His eyes were still open.

"What are you thinking about?" I asked him.

"I don't know," he replied decisively.

"Then go to sleep," I said.

After a few minutes of silence, he turned back to me. "Does Lucifer fly on airplanes?" he asked.

"I don't think so," I replied.

"Then how does he get to places?" he asked.

"He walks," I said. "Now go to sleep."

Pat probably fell asleep thinking about Lucifer. As for me, I fell asleep thinking about the lady in black—the one who came in with the preacher. I had a feeling that while Lucifer might be as bad as they say, that dark lady might be a lot harder to deal with.

CHAPTER FOURTEEN
Lucifer Comes

The next morning I put the truck in neutral and steered it while Father used the tractor to pull it out of Schneider's new lake. Once it was out, he unhitched it and I drove it into our yard and parked it in its usual spot. I affectionately patted the steering wheel before I got out. I had no doubt that next fall I would be driving it full-time, hauling our wheat in from the field.

I was now twelve years old, having reached that milestone a few weeks back, on March eighteenth. I was practically grown up. Poor Pat had just turned eight, lagging behind me by four years and destined to remain in that inferior position for the rest of his life.

After our good clothes had been rescued from the truck and brought into the house, Pat and I went back out on the road in our rubber boots. We waded half the distance across the new lake, which was quite shallow except in the ditches. We even went a little farther into it, until the water was a quarter inch from the brims of our boots. We were born risk takers.

Later on, we moved to a shallow ditch at the bottom of Charlie's hill, where we proceeded to float bits of wood in the pool of water there, pretending they were ships. Suddenly, Bounce let out a muffled yelp. He was standing rigidly in the middle of the road looking up the hill. All at once he reversed direction and took off like a frightened rabbit. We watched him in bewilderment until he disappeared into our driveway.

"He saw something up there," Pat remarked, squinting at the top of the hill.

"There's nothing there," I said dismissively after surveying the hillside.

At first there was nothing. Then a hat appeared, and then the dark shape of a man rose against the sky. He paused for a few seconds, then started down the hill toward us.

He was tall and thin, with a crooked staff in one of his large hands. The fingers of his other hand were knitted through the rope of the bundled poke he was carrying over his shoulder. He wore high boots and he was dressed in dark clothing, with a long, open greatcoat that came down past his knees. He wore a Humphrey Bogart fedora.

It was pulled so far down that it cast a deep shadow over his face.

He paused about halfway down the hill and set his bundle on the ground. As if by magic, a cigarette suddenly dangled from the side of his mouth. He ignited a sulfur match with a flick of his thumbnail and raised it to the cigarette. That's when we got our first good look at what had been hidden in the shadow of the fedora.

I saw a narrow face, a jutting chin, and a small mouth with thin red lips. Above his lips, in the middle of his face, in the place where his nose should have been, there was just a small blob of pink flesh and two adjacent holes.

"He hasn't got a nose," I said in a hoarse voice.

"It's Lucifer," Pat whispered.

We abandoned our boats in the middle of the Pacific Ocean and took off for home. We ran hard because we were anxious to get away from there. We were also anxious to let Mother know that the devil was on the way down our hill.

She was standing at the stove stirring a pot of chicken soup with her long wooden spoon. She turned briefly to smile at us when we burst into the kitchen. I was panting for breath, but Pat had saved enough to get out the good news.

"Lucifer's coming down the hill!" he informed her in one long gasp.

She paused in her stirring of the soup and looked around at us with an irritated expression on her face.

"It's true!" I exclaimed. "We saw him coming down, and he hasn't got a nose!"

After a long, still moment during which Mother contemplated our startling information, the wooden spoon again began to move slowly around in the soup. I had expected some significant reaction from her, but there was none. It was very disappointing.

"I think he's coming here," I said.

"I think it's time you two stopped acting like silly little boys," she responded. "Or else I'm going to tell your father."

"Where is he?" I asked.

"He went to take some things out to the Hermit," she said.

Father would now and then pick up a few supplies for the Hermit, which he would carry out to him in his army knapsack. For reasons we didn't understand, Pat and I were not allowed to go along on these supply trips.

A second later there was a sharp rap at our door. Pat and I immediately ran to the kitchen window and sprawled across the table to look sideways at the stoop.

"It's him!" I exclaimed.

"He still hasn't got a nose," Pat observed.

After a moment of absolute silence, Mother let the wooden spoon rest in the soup pot and wiped her hands on her apron. She went to the door and cracked it open. She spoke to him briefly in a low voice while Pat and I continued to stare through the window at the gaunt, noseless figure.

After Mother closed the door, he turned around and sat down on our stoop.

"He wants something to eat," she said. She was standing with her back to the door, her hands pressed against the doorknob. She was very pale.

"Is it Lucifer?" Pat asked.

"Don't be silly," she said. She quickly threw open the basement hatch and started down the steps to fetch some things from the basement cooler. But she paused on the upper steps and looked back at us.

"Go upstairs and look down the creek to see if your father's on his way back," she said as she disappeared into the darkness below.

We did as we were told, even though I didn't think Father would be on his way back so soon. When he went to see the Hermit, he usually stayed for hours. And when he did get home, he would usually need a big dose of strong coffee and a good night's sleep before he was completely himself again.

We went upstairs and looked south; however, as expected, there was no sign of him. We watched the area closely for a few more minutes. There was still nothing to report, so we returned to the kitchen.

"He isn't coming yet," I informed Mother.

She rolled her eyes, then lifted a plate of chicken sandwiches with one hand and picked up a mug of coffee with the other. She drew in her breath and glanced at us.

"Get the door," she said.

"Do you mean Pat or me?" I asked. We were both looking sideways out the window, so it could have been either of us.

"I mean you," she said to me. "Now open it, and for heaven's sake, don't stare at him."

I opened the door, then jumped back and peered around the edge as she went out onto the stoop. The man stood up at the sound and half turned his head. The brim of the fedora was slanted far down as he accepted the sandwiches and coffee. There was only the merest nod of his long chin, then he sat down on the stoop and began to eat.

I resumed my position at the window next to Pat. The stranger was very hungry. He pushed the sandwiches into his mouth, a quarter at a time.

"I'm watching his chin," Pat informed me.

"Me too," I said.

Actually his chin was about all we could see of his face because his fedora was slanted down in our direction and it hid most of it. However, his chin was interesting enough by itself. It mostly went through long up and down motions as he munched away at his sandwiches, but occasionally it would change direction and swing forcefully from side to side as if it had suddenly become unhinged.

When the last bit of the last sandwich had disappeared into his small mouth, he curled his hand around the coffee mug and began to move.

"He's standing up," Pat reported.

After he stood up, he carefully surveyed the whole extent of our farmyard, turning his head slowly so as not to miss any detail of it.

"He's going down to the barn," I observed.

"Don't stare at him! He might see you," Mother said,

glancing at us from the stove. After a moment of silence, she looked back at us again.

"What's he doing now?" she asked.

"He just put the coffee cup on a fence post," I said. "Now he's walking again, but he's not going to the barn now."

"He's going past the combine," Pat observed.

He went down the wide lane by the barn, past our restored chicken coop, and down to the open woodshed.

"He's at the woodshed," I said.

There he paused for a moment, then he walked over to the stump and pulled our long ax out from it. He ran his thumb back and forth along the edge.

"He picked up our ax," Pat duly reported.

"Bolt the doors," Mother ordered.

Bolting the back door was easy, but the front door presented a bit of a problem.

"The front door doesn't have a bolt," I reminded her.

We lived in an honest part of the country, where one locked door was considered more than sufficient.

"Is he Lucifer?" Pat asked worriedly.

"Go to the front door and get ready to run down the road to the Schneiders' if I tell you to," Mother ordered, her hands fluttering about. "And if I tell you, run with all your might and don't look back until you get there. And when you get there, tell them—"

"He's chopping up our wood," Pat interrupted. He had gone back to the window. I went over to confirm it, and sure enough, Lucifer was chopping our wood for us.

He knew how to wield an ax too, and he worked steadily while all of us watched him from the window. He only paused twice—once to wipe an arm across his face and once to pull his fedora down a little. While we were still watching him Father walked into the yard.

"Father's back," Pat said quite unnecessarily.

"Thank God," Mother responded.

She sighed and left the window to go back to her soup, but Pat and I continued to monitor the events outside.

"Father's seen him," I informed her. "He's walking over to the woodpile. Now he's almost there. Now he's there. Now he's talking to him! Now he's scratching his head. I mean Father is scratching his own head."

"He's coming up and Lucifer's chopping again," Pat reported.

When Father came into the house, Mother was waiting at the door.

"Who is he?" she asked in a worried voice.

"Just a vagrant," Father said calmly. "Nothing to worry about."

"What's a vagrant?" Pat asked.

"A tramp," Father replied. "Someone who wanders around the country because he doesn't have a home."

"He doesn't have a nose either," Pat commented.

"He frightened me," Mother confessed. "He still does. I hope he's leaving right away."

"Actually, I told him he could bed down in the loft for the night," Father informed her.

"Is Lucifer going to sleep in our barn?" Pat asked.

"Pat thinks he's Lucifer," I explained to Father.

Father frowned again. "He's not Lucifer," he said in an irritated voice. "He's just a poor unfortunate looking for a place to sleep and a bit of food to put in his belly before he moves on. And I know what that's like. But the point is, he's got nothing and we've got everything, so we shouldn't begrudge him a little hospitality."

"He hasn't got a nose," Pat pointed out again.

"And we definitely shouldn't judge a person by the way he looks. Understand?" he asked, glowering down at us.

We looked up at him and nodded.

"Mr. Lucifer scared Bounce," Pat reported with a worried look. "He ran away."

"And he hasn't come back," I added.

Father shook his head in a tired way and went over to the washstand.

"I'm as generous as the next person," Mother said from the stove, "but I'm afraid of that man. I don't like his eyes and I don't like his hat. I won't even mention anything else. And I definitely don't want him to stay here," she concluded firmly.

"It's too late," Father replied. "I've told him he could stay in the barn tonight, and I can't go back on my word."

"No," Mother said.

"Yes," Father insisted. "And what's more, we're going to feed him while he's here. It's the least we can do. Look at him work out there."

"Oh, Eddie," Mother moaned. "I've got a bad feeling about that man."

Mother was Irish and she sometimes got bad feelings about people. She was usually right about them too. But as for Pat and me, now that Father was back, we knew we had nothing to fear from the stranger. And I, for one, was very curious to see him up close at our supper table, with his hat off. However, that was not to be. Later when Father went out to fetch him for supper, he returned alone.

"He won't come in the house," he said to Mother.

"That's fine with me," she said cheerfully. "I'll send a nice supper out to him."

It was I who carried his supper plate out to him, while Pat followed closely with the dessert and coffee. Later that night, in bed, we discussed what we'd seen.

"Maybe there's horns under his hat," I said.

"What horns?" Pat asked.

"Lucifer's got horns," I told him. "They grow out of the top of his head."

"What are they for?" Pat asked.

"They're to show how evil he is," I informed him.

"Oh," Pat replied.

After contemplating the information for a moment, he turned his head back in my direction.

"Are cows evil?" he asked.

"Go to sleep," I ordered.

We lay silently for a time, then I closed my eyes. "Maybe he'll come up from the barn and chop us up during the night," I said as we drifted off to sleep.

We made it to morning intact, then we quickly dressed and went outside. There was still no sign of Bounce. We went around calling his name for a while, then gave up on him.

"Will he come back?" Pat asked with tears in his eyes.

"He'll come back when he gets hungry," I reassured him.

We climbed up to the loft and took up a prone position on top of one of the high piles of hay so we could watch Lucifer as he slept down below us. He slept with his hat on, unfortunately, so we were unable to make a determination as to the presence or absence of horns.

"He snores," Pat whispered.

That was true. Mr. Lucifer was snoring just as well as anyone blessed with a complete nose might do. Then he stopped snoring and opened his eyes and looked up at us. We stared at one another for a long moment, then he wiped his absent nose with his sleeve and pulled his fedora lower. He snorted once and sat upright.

"Where do you live?" I asked him.

"Wherever I happen to be," he answered in a hollow voice after clearing his throat.

"Where did you grow up?" I persisted.

"New York City," he muttered as he got to his feet.

"Do you go to church?" I asked.

"Not much," Mr. Lucifer admitted as he rooted in his bundle. He brought out a straight razor and opened it up. After he'd wiped the gleaming blade on his trousers, he slipped it into his pocket.

"We go to church," I said. "But we don't have a minister anymore, because he went to live in Bemidji. But last Sunday the Reverend Kluny preached to us."

"He scared us," Pat added.

Mr. Lucifer didn't reply. He just frowned a little, like he had a slight headache. He got up, took a brush and cup from his little poke, then climbed down the ladder.

We followed Mr. Lucifer down the ladder and padded along behind him over to the horse trough, where we watched him tip his fedora back a little and wash up. When that was done, he made a shaving lather in the cup and brushed it onto his face. He shaved with his hat on, and he didn't even use a mirror.

"We're going to Wistola today," Pat informed him.

"Good-bye," Mr. Lucifer said.

"We're not going yet," Pat said. "We have to have our breakfast first."

"What are you doing way out here?" I asked him in a friendly way. He looked straight at me with his piercing blue eyes and his missing nose.

"I'm trying to shave," he answered.

Mother fed Mr. Lucifer a large breakfast of ham and pancakes, which we carried out to him. He put it on top of a high pile of wood in the woodshed and ate it standing up. We watched him go at it until Mother called us back to the house. After we'd finished our own breakfast, we ran back to the woodshed to see how Mr. Lucifer was making out with his. He was just finishing up when we got there.

"I like pancakes," Pat informed him. "Do you like pancakes?"

"Not much," he muttered. "I thought you were going somewhere."

We were, but it was still too early to leave, so we hung around and watched him smoke a cigarette. We particularly liked to watch the smoke come out through the two holes where his nose would have been, if he'd had one. Then Mother called us in to get our good clothes on. When we left him, Mr. Lucifer was sitting on the chopping block staring hard at the barn.

"Mr. Lucifer's hardly got any teeth left," Pat said when we came into the house.

"How many times do I have to tell you!" Father exclaimed hotly. "He's not Mr. Lucifer! He's just a man!"

"What's his name?" Mother inquired.

"You know, I never asked him," Father admitted. "We never even shook hands, come to think of it."

"It's just as well," she said. "I hope he leaves today."

"Have a little charity, Kathleen." Father glowered. "He's just a poor fellow trying to get by, that's all."

"Well, I don't trust him," Mother declared. "And I certainly don't like leaving him here alone. He could steal us blind and take off for the hills before we get back."

"You're being suspicious for no reason," Father said with a frown.

"Better to be a little suspicious than a lot sorry," she muttered.

"Look, Kathleen, I spent over four years in the army,

so I think I know a little more about men than you do," Father declared.

We went into Wistola and saw Mrs. Windemere because Mother had heard she was sick. When we got there, she was eating chocolates in bed and didn't seem to be very sick at all. Before we returned home, we went to a movie called *The Yearling*, which was about a boy and his deer and a horrible bear. It was a great movie. Pat cried in it, and I came close to it myself. When we returned to the farm, we were surprised and happy to find that Bounce had returned. He bounded all around the yard, greeting us with joyous barks.

"I've got a hunch our visitor's gone," Father commented.

We went out to the barn and discovered that Goldie had had her calf while we were away. Father shook his head as he looked at the new calf.

"If I'd thought she was that far along, I wouldn't have left her alone," he said.

"What about Mr. Lucifer?" Pat asked.

"Go take a look," Father said.

Pat and I climbed up to the loft. There wasn't a trace of Mr. Lucifer up there, and his bundle was gone.

"He's gone!" Pat and I shouted down.

At the same time we yelled the news, we both saw something gleaming under the hay. Pat went over and picked it up, and we stared at it with amazement. It was Auntie Margaret's Eleanor Roosevelt pie pan. With Pat right behind me, I leaped down the ladder and held it up for them to see. Mother took the pie pan in her hand and examined it closely.

"It's definitely Margaret's," she said. "I'd know it anywhere."

"Did Mr. Lucifer steal Auntie Margaret's pie?" Pat asked.

"It looks like it," Father replied. "But stop calling him Mr. Lucifer. How many times do I have to tell you?"

"Well, we'd better go change our clothes," Mother suggested.

"Yeah," Father agreed.

We took a final look at our new calf and headed out.

"Well anyway, Margaret will be glad to get her pie pan back," Mother commented as we emerged from the barn.

"Yeah," Father said. "Funny thing that. Him coming to this particular farm and leaving that pan behind. I mean he couldn't know we were related to Margaret. Just a coincidence, I guess."

Mother led the way inside but stopped short and stared at the kitchen table.

"He took the apple pie we were going to have for supper," she said. "Oh! It was in my Pennsbury pie pan!"

"Well, you'll just have to make do without it," Father replied easily.

"You're being way too charitable, if you ask me," she said. "I just wonder what else he took." She raised her eyebrows at him, then went into the living room.

"Your mother's the suspicious type," Father said with a wink.

While he was over at the water pail filling the coffeepot, she came back from the living room. She was not smiling.

"He's emptied our piggy bank," she said. "A dollar and thirty-five cents. All gone."

"Well, that's too bad," Father admitted. "But it's little enough when you think about it. We'll just write it off to charity." After setting the coffeepot on the stove, he lit his pipe and calmly sat down at the table. All the while, she just stared at him.

"He also took that unopened bottle of whiskey that Danny left for you," she informed him.

"Why, the dirty rotten devil!" Father roared, smoke billowing out of his nose.

A few minutes later Father, Pat, and I piled into the truck and took off in search of the villain. We went up and down all the roads around there, but we didn't see him. No one else in the vicinity had seen him either. Mr. Lucifer had simply vanished from the face of the earth, along with Mother's Pennsbury pie pan and our piggy-bank savings. And of course, Father's bottle of twelve-year-old whiskey.

CHAPTER FIFTEEN
Love Story

Andy Sims was a little slow on the uptake. However, in spite of a couple of failures along the way, he managed to stay in school. He succeeded only because of a lot of extra help from his mother, and because of his own determination and hard work. About Andy you could definitely say that he made the most of what he was given. No one can do better than that.

One afternoon Miss Scott asked him to come up to the front and read out loud a story he'd written all by himself. Andy proudly went up there, scribbler in hand, and started to read his story. He was a little nervous, but with Miss Scott's encouragement he was slowly getting through it.

"And we sitted down at the table," Andy read.

There was a brief pause and Andy looked up, sensing something was wrong with his sentence. At this point Axel could no longer restrain himself, and he laughed out loud at Andy. Axel's mocking laughter was short-lived, however, because Miss Scott came storming down the aisle like the angel of death, and she took Axel by the ear and threw him out of the classroom. He spent the rest of the afternoon smoldering away in the cloakroom by himself—much to the delight of those of us who, like Andy, had suffered from his mockery.

I'd always liked Miss Scott, but never so much as I did on that particular afternoon. On the way home on the bus, there was considerable jubilation because Axel had finally got what he deserved.

The set for our operetta included a large pirate ship. It had been constructed by the townsfolk and set up in the church, and on Friday afternoon we marched over there and did a full rehearsal. It turned out to be a pretty rough-and-ready exercise. One of the tiny pirates fell off the ship in the middle of Nurse Ruth's first song. There were several other misadventures as well, and Miss Scott was not pleased with the way the rehearsal went. As for me, even though I sang my part with smooth perfection, the result of endless hours of practice, she said my overall performance lacked gusto. She said I had to demonstrate what she called "energy and verve," like I was a real pirate king. I was very disappointed with her verdict. I thought I had reached the point of absolute perfection.

On the way home on the bus, it suddenly came to me. All I had to do was move and act like Errol Flynn did when he played Robin Hood in the movie. Just do it that way while singing my heart out and I would become a pirate king no one would ever forget.

When I got home, I sang my song to the pigs, as I always did. After the feeding and singing were over, I found a nice length of lath in the woodpile, and it became my Pirate King sword. With my flashing sword, I went behind the chicken coop, where I sliced the air into small pieces and leaped about in a triumphant Robin Hood manner, all the while singing the "Pirate King Song" with all the force I could muster. I could feel the air all around me swelling up with discharged gusto.

I practiced off and on all weekend, and by Monday I was prepared to play my part with real verve and gusto—ready to move and leap energetically, and to sing and shout like I was really the king of the pirates. We were scheduled to have another rehearsal on Monday afternoon, and I was definitely looking forward to it. Unfortunately, there was no rehearsal, because Miss Scott wasn't there. She was in the hospital in Wistola, getting her tonsils out, and Mrs. Thorne—the doctor's wife—had taken over the school-room during her absence.

Poor old Mrs. Thorne wasn't a teacher, and it showed.

Things did not go smoothly, either in the classroom or out. For some of the kids, it was as if every rule in the school had been thrown out the window. As for me, I sincerely hoped that Miss Scott would get well before the school came apart at the seams. Even if she'd noticed what was going on around her, Mrs. Thorne wouldn't have been able to control the class.

The noise in the classroom was continuous, but it didn't bother Mrs. Thorne, because she was fairly deaf. This was clear from the way she answered questions. When Maria Gonzalez asked her why the moon goes around the earth, Mrs. Thorne's reply was "I believe our month of June got its name from Juno, who was one of the gods of ancient Greece. Or was it ancient Rome? Oh my, I do tend to mix them up. They're very close together, you know. Rome and Greece. If you look at a map, you'll see. Oh dear, where does she keep her maps?"

Outside the school the most important rule of all was broken during the first recess of the first day of Miss Scott's absence when, on the far side of the caragana hedge, a fight broke out between two grade twos. Henry Adamson broke it up before any damage was done.

Halfway through our second tumultuous morning with Mrs. Thorne, I was heading for the pencil sharpener when Axel appeared in front of me. As we were passing he deliberately hit me with his shoulder. I'd had about all I could stand from him, and I gave him a push in return. Unfortunately, I pushed him harder than I meant to and he went backward over Wanda's desk and landed in the adjacent aisle. Even though he deserved what he got, I had a sinking feeling in my heart as I watched him get to his feet. I was not the kind of person who looks for trouble, but I knew I'd just found a truckload of it.

Everyone in the classroom was staring at us as Axel and I confronted each other across the row of desks—everyone except Mrs. Thorne. She was still writing on the blackboard, completely oblivious to what was going on.

"Easy, guys," Henry said from his place.

Axel brushed his hands off on his chest, then he looked across the row and smiled at me as though I'd done him a favor.

"See you at noon, chump," he said.

At first I didn't understand what he meant, but when he clenched his bony fist and held it up for me to look at, I understood. At that same instant I also realized that when I pushed him back and sent him flying, I'd done exactly what he'd wanted me to do. I'd given him the excuse he needed to punch me silly and humiliate me all over again.

I knew that Axel intended to beat me to a pulp. As for me, I had no wish to fight him—or anyone else, for that matter. But if I had to fight him, I would fight him with all my might. I'd make him pay for everything he'd done to me. At least, that's what I told myself. But every now and then for the rest of the morning, my hands would reach up of their own accord and feel my nose, just to make sure it was securely fastened to my face. And every time I thought about what was going to happen to me at noon, a hot, prickly sensation swept over me. I didn't want to get hurt, but the thing I was most afraid of was that I might turn out to be a powder puff—that I would disgrace myself in the fight. There's nothing worse than being humiliated by someone you hate.

I left my lunch behind when I headed outside at noon. I couldn't eat anything anyway. I expected Axel to be waiting nearby when I came out the door, and I assumed we would go behind the caragana bushes to have our fight. I also thought that maybe Henry Adamson might stop the fight before it got going, like he did with the little kids.

But what good would that do? I wondered. *Axel will get me sooner or later. It's better to get it over with right now.*

When I stepped outside, Axel was nowhere in sight, but Emmanuel and Martin were there.

"He's waiting for you behind the meat market," Martin said.

Henry won't be around to stop the fight was my first thought.

"Okay," I said glumly.

They grabbed my arms above my elbows and started to guide me to the front of the school.

"What are you doing?" I protested.

"Making sure you don't chicken out and run away," Martin replied.

"You don't need to drag me there," I said hotly. "I'm not going to run away."

They let me go, and we walked down the street together,

with one of them on either side of me just in case I had second thoughts. But I would sooner have been killed than be labeled a coward.

When we reached the back alley behind the stores, I could see a large group of kids waiting halfway down, behind Haskaine's meat market. For a second my breathing stopped and a tingling sensation swept through me, like there were a million little bubbles bursting in my bloodstream. I felt my knees go weak, but I managed to stay up and go forward.

As we approached the crowd I felt like I was an actor caught up in some kind of strange play that I couldn't escape from—a play starring Axel and Donald. A long time ago I'd dreamed that I was an actor in a play, but when I got onstage, I couldn't remember my lines. No matter how hard I tried, I couldn't remember them, and the whole dream was about worry and shame. At least in this play I didn't have to worry about my lines.

When I arrived behind the meat market, the crowd quickly formed a circle around Axel and me.

"Ready?" Axel said in a friendly voice. He actually seemed to be enjoying himself.

When he raised his fists, I automatically raised mine. My last real thought was simply a vague hope that I wouldn't disgrace myself.

We circled around each other—rather, he circled around me and I turned to follow him, like a sunflower turns with the sun. For what seemed like a long time, nothing happened, and it occurred to me that I could use my archery experience to help me. I looked at him and imagined his face was the target and my arm and fist were my arrow. I then boldly struck out at him, but I missed. He instantly returned the favor, and his fist bounced off the top of my forehead.

For a second just then, I saw two Axels in front of me, both grinning.

That didn't work, I thought.

Clearly, Axel was a much better boxer than I was, and I had a sinking feeling that I was about to be taken apart. I also had the unhappy notion that he was planning to do it slowly, so that I would have to endure the maximum amount of pain and humiliation. I then did something so unexpected that even I wasn't expecting it. I hurled myself straight at him like a blundering rhinoceros, with my fists flying in all directions.

I'm not sure whether I hit him with my fists or not, but I did collide head-on with him and we hit the ground together like a ton of dropped bricks. I wound up on top, but I wasn't there for long. In a split second he reversed our positions and I was flat on my back with his hand on my throat. An instant later his fist was on its way down, moving at high velocity. It was aimed at my face, but I managed to dodge it by twisting my head. On the second try the fist just grazed my cheek. I tried with all my might to throw him off, but I couldn't. I was strong for my age, but he was stronger.

Out of nowhere a large shadow appeared above us, and I saw a galvanized-metal garbage can lid coming down from the sky. It smashed against the top of Axel's skull like Thor's hammer. Axel's fist faltered in midair and went limp. At the same time, his other hand fell away from my throat. He had a blank look in his eyes, as though his brain had been transported into never-never land.

My cousin Annie held the other end of the lid.

"What?" Axel murmured in a strange, disconnected voice. Then he fell off me and rolled over on the ground.

While Annie was helping me up, Axel crawled away on his hands and knees. When his friends managed to get him on his feet, he wobbled forward a little and looked blankly all around, as though he was trying to figure out which way was up.

The back door of the meat market opened suddenly, and Stanley Haskaine appeared in the doorway wearing his blood-splattered butcher's apron. Stanley was a huge, bull-like man, and he was not the friendly sort of butcher who gives free wieners to kids.

"What are you little beggars doing out here?" he growled at us.

We all backed away from him.

Then Stanley spotted his garbage can lid lying on the ground. He picked it up and stared at it with disbelief. The lid had a large dent in it.

"My lid!" he bellowed. "It was brand-new!"

His shout sent shock waves through the air, and like a pile of leaves scattering before a mighty wind, everyone fled up the alley. Emmanuel and Martin had Axel by his upper arms, and they dragged him along behind the rest of us.

"That's it!" Stanley screamed after us. "Hit the road, you bums! Hit the road!"

As we left the alley and headed for the school we heard one final, distant cry from him: "You've ruined it!" he screamed. "It doesn't fit anymore!"

I came out of the fight feeling pretty good—almost happy, in a giddy sort of way. It was as if I'd been through the Charge of the Light Brigade and, much to my surprise, discovered that I had ridden past the Russian cannon and I was still alive. However, although I didn't know it then, one of my eyes was turning black. That night when I got home, Mother noticed it immediately.

"What happened?" she asked.

"He was in a fight," Pat answered for me.

"A fight? I don't like you fighting," she said. "And now you've got another black eye. Heavens to Betsy! One more of those and that eye is going to fall out!"

"Will his eye really fall out?" Pat asked her.

"Yes," she said. "And when it does, his brain will collapse."

"What was it about?" Father asked me.

"It was Axel," I said. Those few words explained everything. He knew all about Axel. They both did.

"Did he start it?" he asked.

"Yes," I said.

"I don't care who started it. I still don't like it," Mother said.

"A guy has to defend himself," Father countered. "Give in to them and they walk all over you. Look at Hitler."

"You look at him," Mother said. "I don't like wars, and I don't like fighting."

"Annie bashed Axel with a garbage can lid," Pat informed them.

"Annie? What's Annie got to do with it?" Mother asked.

"She hit him with this big garbage can lid," Pat went on. "Bam! She really hit him. It made a big dent in it, and Axel went all wobbly. Then the butcher man came out and yelled at us and..."

And on and on he went, until they knew every detail of what happened.

When Pat finally came to the end of it, they looked at each other.

"That's Annie, all right," Father said.

"I don't like it one bit," Mother responded. "If she attacks boys with garbage cans at her age, what's she going to be like when she grows up?"

"I don't know," Father admitted, "but it should be interesting."

When I arrived at school the next day, there was a little surprise waiting for me. Axel had a black eye too. Only his was on the right and mine was on the left.

Of course, everyone in the school knew about the fight, even those who weren't there, but I was slightly disappointed to discover that they weren't interested in how I'd bravely stood up to Axel. All they were talking about was how Annie had lambasted Axel with Mr. Haskaine's garbage can lid.

I expected Axel to pick another fight with me right away. I thought he would try to finish me off before Miss Scott returned from her tonsils operation, but he completely ignored me. I was very content with that—though I didn't understand it. And then to further confound me, he did something quite puzzling.

When school was over, he came around to the front of the building with his pals Martin and Emmanuel, and they congregated next to the pipe-rail fence, where all of us farm kids were waiting for our bus. They then began to play mumbly-peg with a pocketknife. It was strange. It was puzzling. I wondered if maybe he was trying to threaten me with a knife.

I watched them out of the corner of my eye, and I noticed that Axel didn't seem to be paying much attention to the mumbly-peg game. He spent a lot of time looking in our direction. At first I thought he was looking at me, but eventually I discovered that he wasn't watching me at all. He was watching Annie. I wondered if he was trying to scare her by playing with a knife. But that didn't make sense either. Anyone who knew Annie at all would know that sort of thing would never work with her.

Things came to a head the next day at noon. I was walking over to the boys' outhouse when I saw him running toward me. My immediate thought was *This is it. He's going to pulverize me.*

"Don, wait," he yelled.

I stopped dead in my tracks. It was the first time he'd ever called me by my proper name. I was flabbergasted. Then he smiled hesitantly and said, "Does your cousin like me?"

"What?"

"Annie...Does she like me?"

"I don't know," I replied.

"Well, could you find out?" he asked.

"She hit you on the head with a garbage can lid," I reminded him, thinking it might answer his question.

"I know," he said, "but that was when I was beating you up. So maybe when I'm not beating you up, she likes me."

I looked closely at him, and I saw that his eyes were all aglow. And suddenly I understood.

He was in love with Annie.

As Father often said: "There are more strange people in this world, Horatio, than you'll ever dream of."

My first impulse was to feel sorry for him.

That day as the bus rolled homeward I sat down next to Annie and asked her the critical question—a question that could have a lot to do with my future welfare. I calculated that if Axel was in love with Annie, and if Annie loved him back—or, at least, if she liked him a bit—then since she was my blood relative, Axel would probably never bother me again.

"Axel wants to know if you like him," I asked her. I spoke in a serious and somewhat hopeful voice. She gave me a strange look and her brow furrowed. I didn't think she understood the question, so I repeated it.

"Axel wants to know if you like him," I said.

"I heard you the first time," she said.

She was evidently considering the question carefully. Finally, she looked at me and spoke the words I was hoping not to hear.

"Tell him I hate his guts," she said. "Now go away. I want to read my book."

"It's my book," I pointed out. "And I want it back when you're finished with it."

The next morning Axel was waiting for me when the bus rolled in. Annie passed by him first, but she walked on by without so much as a glance in his direction. His eyes followed her as she went, then they anxiously turned to me.

"Did you ask her? What did she say?" he asked me eagerly as we walked together around the side of the school.

Ever since yesterday I'd been thinking about how to answer this question. I knew the best thing is to always tell the truth, but I'd decided I'd work toward it in a gradual fashion.

"She likes you a little," I said.

"She does?"

His face lit up. Once again his eyes were all aglow, and once again I felt sorry for him.

"Yes, she does," I said. "A little. But she'd like you better if you were nicer to people," I informed him.

He had a faraway look in his eye as he turned away and wandered off. I heard a slight moan as he went, and I was amazed at what love had done to him.

A few days later I was sitting on the pipe-rail fence out front, reading a dull book under a gray sky, when I noticed that Axel and his friends were about to pass by Hannah on the sidewalk. I expected the usual "Sunshine Mountain" joke, but as they approached, Axel smiled at her in a friendly fashion.

"Hi, Hannah," he said.

Hannah clearly hadn't expected any sort of greeting from Axel, certainly not a friendly one. For a second she had a puzzled expression on her face, then her eyes warmed and she smiled at him as only she could smile.

"What did you do that for?" Emmanuel asked him.

"Mind your own business," Axel growled at him.

That same day, I came around the corner of the school just in time to see Emmanuel angrily confronting Annie about something.

"He's changed!" Emmanuel cried. "Ever since you hit him with that garbage can lid, he isn't the same. He's gone all gooey. You damaged his brain!"

Emmanuel's face was red with anger, and his eyes glittered with hate. Annie stared back at him with ice in her eyes.

"You're next," she said in a low voice that sent shivers down my spine.

One starry Saturday night in May, the church was packed to the gunnels and we were assembled and ready to perform *The Pirates of Penzance*. I was steaming with pent-up gusto, ready to blast them away with my performance. A few minutes later I was on the stage singing "Pour, Oh Pour the Pirate Sherry" with my pirate band.

I threw all my heart and soul into my portrayal of the Pirate King—not just the singing either. At every opportunity I leaped around in a pretty good imitation of Robin Hood of Locksley. I even did a few unrehearsed leaps, which would have been quite spectacular if I hadn't hurt my ankle. Fortunately, the injury came near the end, and I was able to stay onstage until it was over, despite the pain. Afterward Miss Scott looked at my ankle and said it wasn't broken. She also said that I got what I deserved for showing off. And then for some reason, she broke into a spasm of laughter that showed no respect for my injury. And it didn't stop until I'd hobbled away from her.

When the show was over, the audience was very happy with our performance. How could they not be, since we all belonged to them? Miss Scott was less enthusiastic, however, because one of the tiny pirates had fallen off the larboard side of our pirate ship. Falling off wasn't so bad, but the problem was that he did it early on, in the middle of Nurse Ruth's song, and it caused so much laughter and commotion among the audience that most of her song was lost in the noisy air. It would have been better if Nurse Ruth had stopped singing when it happened, and then started over after the audience had quieted down. But she didn't. She plowed on, right through it. Hannah was playing the part of Ruth, and the pirate standing next to her said that she swore under her breath when it happened.

Interrupting a song is one thing—not good at any

time—but this particular song was essential to understanding the plot. The result was that the audience didn't have a clue what our operetta was all about.

I thought my overall performance was fairly magnificent, in spite of the bad leap, but no one mentioned it to me afterward, except for Rachel, my parents, and my aunt and uncle. The fact is, everyone was talking about Billy Shapiro's performance as General Stanley, and how brilliantly he'd done the "Modern Major-General Song." I guess he did it pretty well, although it isn't really so much a song as it is a lot of fast talking—which was something Billy was good at.

The next morning when I was feeding the pigs, my father came out of the house with his coffee in hand. He walked over to the pigpen and leaned on the fence, watching me work. When I came out, we walked back to the house together. We'd be off to church in a little while, and for the first time in a long time, I wanted to go. I wanted to sing in the choir and just be there.

"Your mother and I are proud of you," Father said as we approached the back steps. "Let's sit down for a minute," he suggested.

He sat down, and I sat down beside him. I looked at the barn and the other buildings, at the new garden and the blue sky above it all. He put his arm around my shoulders and gave me a pat.

Later on in the morning when I was sitting on the benches with the rest of the church choir and Mr. Winkfeld was reading one of Saint Paul's letters to the Corinthians,

I began to wonder about the Corinthians. They seemed to come up fairly often on Sundays, and yet I didn't have the faintest idea who they were. I looked out at the faces of the congregation and wondered if they knew.

While I was gazing at the congregation it occurred to me that these were the same people who had witnessed my humiliation last August. It didn't matter anymore. My memory of it had faded away, and so had theirs. A lot had happened since then, both good and bad. I knew a lot more now. I'd gone through so much and I'd done so much—archery, truck driving, skiing, struggling against arithmetic, dancing, singing, acting, and defending myself. The main thing was that I felt like myself again. The wretched version of me who thought his life was ruined forever because he missed a catch out in left field was gone. My only regret was that I couldn't play ball anymore, because I'd taken an oath against it.

CHAPTER SIXTEEN
The Best Game in Town

I had no use for the first baseman's mitt Uncle Danny had given me, so on Monday I took it to school in a bag. At lunchtime I gave it to Henry Adamson for the teams to use. Ever since I'd dropped out of baseball, I'd felt a slight coldness in Henry's gaze whenever he looked at me. But that coldness vanished entirely when I handed my brand-new Spalding first baseman's mitt over to him. He immediately insisted that I rejoin the team.

"I can't," I said.

"Well, if you change your mind, you know where we are," he said as he headed for the ball field.

After he'd gone, Miss Scott walked over to me. "Don't you want to play baseball anymore?" she asked me.

"I want to, but I can't. I gave my word that I wouldn't, and I can't go back on my word."

"I admire you for wanting to keep your word. It's a good thing. But what does it actually mean when you give your word?"

I looked at her, not understanding what she was getting at.

"It means you've made a promise, doesn't it?" she said. "A promise to someone—or to yourself, in this case."

"Yes," I agreed.

"There are times when we make promises in haste," she said. "Silly promises. It happens to everyone."

I nodded. That's exactly what I'd done.

"When you make a silly promise to someone, you are free to ask them to absolve you from your promise. If they're willing to do that, then the promise is called off honorably."

I'd never thought of it that way, and it sounded reasonable to me. "But I made the promise to myself."

"Same thing," she said. "If you're willing to admit that it was a silly promise, then you have the power to absolve yourself from it. The only condition is that you try not to make silly promises in the future."

"I won't," I said.

As soon as she left, I absolved myself of my promise and headed out to the ball field. Henry smiled broadly when I made my appearance. "Welcome back," he said.

Following his instructions, I grabbed a glove and took up the vacant shortstop spot on the Blue team. There were a couple of teasing comments from a few of the kids, but I had learned my lesson. I just ignored them. There were none from Axel. He wasn't bothering me anymore at all. Nor, thankfully, was he bothering anyone else. Just Annie.

My first time at bat I hit a low fly toward first base. Vincent reached out and easily caught it with my first baseman's mitt, and he put me out. Without the mitt he probably would have missed it. I didn't care. The only thing I cared about was that I was playing baseball again.

One day we were short a man, and I wound up playing in my old position in left field. During the game I made a long throw that went right into Henry's glove at home plate, and it arrived in time to get the out.

"That was a nice throw," he said afterward. "You've improved from last year, that's for sure."

I took his compliment to heart. Henry never praised anyone unless they really deserved it. I wondered if all the hours and hours of archery practice had something to do with it. Perhaps it had strengthened my arm and improved my reflexes and aim.

One day while I was waiting for the bus Henry came over and loaned me an old baseball and a couple of spare gloves. "You've got a good arm, Donnie," he said. "If you practice enough, you might make pitcher next year."

I might make pitcher next year! I was aglow with the

idea all the way home, and I vowed to practice every free moment I had.

Pat was happy to play catch with me when we got home, but his fingers were made of butter. On my very first throw, the ball went right through his gloved hand, and a split second later Bounce scooped it up from the ground. Pat called at him to bring it back to us, but Bounce didn't seem to understand what he was supposed to do. He just stood there staring at Pat, the ball sticking out of the side of his mouth like a gigantic white boil. Then when Pat started over to take the ball from him, he backed up. He didn't want to give it up. A stick he would always return. A ball was something different, it seemed. I told Pat to stand back, and I smiled at Bounce.

"Good boy," I said. "Bring it to me. That's a good boy. Bring it here, Bounce. Come on, Bounce. Here, Bounce. Good boy. Bring me the ball."

But Bounce just stood there in the middle of the lane with our ball in his mouth.

"You stupid dog," I said under my breath.

I took a few gentle steps toward him; however, as with Pat, he backed away as I approached. I decided the situation called for a different tactic. An ambush.

"You keep talking to him and I'll circle around behind," I said.

Pat dutifully began to coax Bounce to bring the ball to him in order to keep Bounce's attention fixed on him. Meanwhile, I quietly slipped behind the machine shed and crept out the other side so I could jump him from behind. I got behind him okay, but just as I was about to leap on him, he sensed my presence and ran away.

We chased him between the machine shed and the chicken coop and across the near pasture. We chased him into the woods. We chased him through the woods and into the far pasture and back into the woods again, until we lost sight of him. Having been raised properly by upright, caring parents, I never swore. However, I'd never before been so severely provoked.

"What does that word mean?" Pat asked me.

"Never mind," I said, "but don't say it when Mother's around. If you do, don't tell her you got it from me."

As we were making our way out of the woods we saw him. He was behind some bushes about twenty feet away, on our left. He was just standing there watching us, with the ball in his mouth. Then I had another idea.

"Don't move," I warned Pat.

I went slowly backward, away from the dog, until I located a chunk of wood. I waved it at him, and then I threw it with all my might while screaming, "Bounce, go fetch. Fetch!"

Aside from eating, chasing chunks of wood was the thing Bounce liked to do best. And sure enough, just as I'd hoped, he took off after it. When he got to it, he dropped the ball in favor of the chunk of wood, which he immediately brought to us. I threw it as far away as I could, and he went after it again.

We ran to recover the ball and discovered that it was thoroughly coated with dog slime. Pat refused to have anything to do with it, so I had to pick it up myself. In the meantime, Bounce returned with the chunk of wood. I threw it as far into the woods as I could and he disappeared again. After I'd washed the ball off in the trough, we resumed our practice.

I missed Pat's very first throw because he threw it over my head. When I turned around to get it, I was just in time to see a black-and-white streak dart out of the woods, grab the ball in its mouth, and run off with it.

I uttered a small cry of despair.

He ran down the lane, then turned and waited patiently for us to chase him. I went into the woods, found another stick of wood, and recovered the ball. Fortunately, Bounce preferred chasing sticks to hanging around with a baseball in his mouth. When he brought the stick back this time, we seized him and tied him to a tree deep in the woods, out of our sight.

We had just resumed our practice when Mother rang the bell for supper. During the first hour of my ardent quest to become a pitcher I'd managed two practice throws.

After supper, and after again tying Bounce to a tree in the woods, we played catch for an hour or so, until Pat got tired of it. Then I pitched to my father for a little while, until the magnetic force of the tractor pulled him away from me. Later on, Mother got into the act, and I was surprised to discover how good she was at it. Maybe baseball really did run in the family.

That night in bed, just when I was warm and comfortable, I realized that Bounce wasn't at the bottom of our bed, where he normally slept. *Oh no,* I thought. *Poor Bounce. He's still tied to that tree.* My heart sank. I leaped out of bed, lit the trouble lantern, and rushed outside to untie him. I hadn't stopped to put a coat on, and the rain bucketed down on me as I ran toward the woods.

"I'm sorry, Bounce," I said as I released him from the tree. He was all wet and shivering. I quickly took him into the house and led him over to the kitchen stove. I ran to fetch some old towels, then began to briskly rub him down and dry him off. He seemed to appreciate the attention, encouraging me every now and then with a small flurry of kisses on my face. I kept at it until he was as dry and warm as I could make him, then I looked after myself. When we were both dry and warm, we went upstairs together and I settled him in his place at the bottom of the bed. He seemed to have recovered from his ordeal. I sat beside him on the bed, stroking his head and talking to him in a comforting voice. When I saw that he was falling asleep, I turned out the lamp and crawled into bed next to Pat.

In the days that followed, as soon as we got home from school, my brother and I would usually play catch along the lane until the bell summoned us for supper. Sometimes when Father had a few minutes to spare, Pat and I went out to the pasture behind the chicken coop with him so he could bat some flies out to us. We didn't have a real bat, but he had trimmed down an old barrel stave and it worked well enough.

When Pat was unavailable and there was no one else to catch for me, I threw the ball at my archery straw bales, with a tin can stuffed in the middle as a target. The exercise reminded me of archery, except it wasn't as much fun. For one thing, I spent most of my time walking back and forth to retrieve the ball. If I'd had four or five baseballs, it would have been tolerable.

In my daydreams I imagined that I was playing in the big leagues, like my uncle nearly did. In my dreams I became rich and famous.

Pat's interest in baseball had grown ever since Father and Mother had taken us into town to watch a game between the Station Hill Sodbusters and the Melody Patriots. As a result, he was getting better at catching my throws. One day when we were playing catch, I complimented him on his improvement. "You're getting pretty good," I said when he picked a high throw out of the air. He smiled at me.

"If I die," he said, "you can have my telescope."

"If I die, you can have my archery set," I responded. "If you're careful with it," I added.

The supper bell rang and we headed back to the house. We were met by our parents at the bottom of the steps. Mother was holding something behind her back, and the two of them were all smiles.

"We bought you a little present," Father informed us.

"What is it?" Pat asked, whereupon Mother's hand emerged from behind her back. It contained a brand-new baseball.

"Catch," she said to Pat.

"No!" I cried.

It was too late. She'd already thrown it to Pat with a gentle underhand.

The ball never reached him. There was a flash of black and white, and the ball was snatched out of the air. Bounce ran off a little distance, then turned and looked at us with our new baseball sticking out of his mouth.

"Here, Bounce. Bring it here," Mother urged him. Bounce merely looked at her.

I turned toward Pat. "Go get a stick," I said.

Two weeks later school was over and we were on the bus, opening the brown envelopes that contained our final report cards. Miss Scott was the kind of teacher who'd fail her own mother if she didn't measure up, so when it came to report cards, the smell of danger was always in the air. When I opened mine, it was a considerable relief to discover that I had been advanced to grade seven. What's more, except for math my grades had improved a little. But although moving ahead a grade was nice, the most important thing about the conclusion of the school year was that I was firmly established in the shortstop position, and I loved it.

A few seats down from me, my brother was announcing that he was now in grade three. Next year he'd be playing baseball too, and at last we'd have something in common besides having the same parents.

It had turned into a good year, after all. My humiliation in the game with Melody was forgotten by everyone, and just a distant memory for me. What's more, because of that humiliation I'd become an expert archer, which had, in turn, improved my throwing arm. So Miss Scott was right when she said, "Out of every failure a greater success can come, although it may come from another direction."

I still had to feed the pigs morning and night, but other than that, things were looking pretty good. The glorious summer vacation was here, our crop was doing fine, I was practicing my pitching every day, and the miracle of electricity was coming soon to make our life even richer than it already was.